FINDING ME,

Finding You

FINDING ME,

Finding You

DONNA HODGES

Dallas, Texas

Published by Higgins Publishing

Higgins Publishing is committed to excellence in the publishing industry. The company reflects the philosophy established by the founder, based on Psalm 68:11, *"The Lord gave the word and great was the company of those who published it."*

Book design Copyright © 2017 by Higgins Publishing. All Rights Reserved.
Cover design by Higgins Publishing

The Higgins Publishing Speakers Bureau provides a wide range of authors for speaking events. To schedule an author for an event, go to higginspublishing.com.

Library of Congress Cataloging-in-Publication Data Control Number: 2016954475   February 2017
Brown, Donna
Finding Me, Finding You
Donna Brown – Higgins Publishing 1st Revised Edition   February 2024
pages cm. 284
ISBN: 978-1-941580-58-5 (sc)
ISBN: 978-1-941580-59-2 (eb)

1. General / Family and Relationships
2. Self-Help / Self-Improvement / Motivational

For information about special discounts for bulk purchases, subsidiary, foreign and translations rights & permissions, please contact Higgins Publishing at, contact@higginspublishing.com.

Published in the United States of America

More From Donna Hodges

Find at Higgins Publishing, Amazon, Barnes & Noble,

And Wherever Books Are Sold!

Dedications

First and far most, I thank God for placing this book on my heart back in 2010 and for giving me the opportunity to release it finally. He gave me three months to write it but then, He wouldn't allow me to release it because it wasn't complete. I still had so much more that has happened in my life that I needed to add. So, Lord, Thank You, for keeping me patient these past six years.

I dedicate this book to my loving mother, Annie Wright who lost her life to Diabetes in January 2002.

I also would like to dedicate this book to my baby brother, Christopher Potter who lost his life on March 29, 1972, to pneumonia. He was only seven months old.

To my children, Stephen A. Brown and Darius L. Brown who are the center of my joy. Without the love and support of these two young men, I would never have been able to accomplish what I have today. Their love and support have allowed me to travel without wondering if they regretted me being the author that I am. I love them so much.

To my loving husband, Terry Hodges, I don't know what I would have done without you in my life. You may have come to me in my mid-forties, but for a short period of my life, you have shown me the kind of love that I've never experienced before. The day you almost lost your life, mine would have shattered forever. I thank God for keeping you on this side of the Earth. Thank you so much, honey, for being a vital part of my life.

To my father, Mr. James Wright, I thank you for being there for me when I needed a comforting shoulder to lean on, for allowing me to be a part of your seventieth birthday, and for allowing me to take you places you've never been before. I love you, daddy.

To my stepdaughters, Stephanie and Britney Hodges, thank you for allowing me to be a part of your father's world and for accepting me into your family. I love you both so very much.

To my family, friends, and fans, I would not be where I am without your support. A very special thank you to my Uncle, David Wright who is like a father to me. My Aunt and Uncle Raymond Jones who sheltered, clothed and accepted me into their house at 16, Daisy King for being like a sister I've never had, Larry McDowell, Joyce Harley, Rodney Wellington, and Nicos Brown for inspiring me to write the many novels that I have.

To my cousin, Shanene Higgins, thank you for giving me this opportunity to share my life with the world. I am so grateful and glad we connected.

Table of Contents

Prologue

Finding Me, Finding You

DONNA AND PORTUGUESE

From the day that I was born, I used to believe I was a gluten for pain. I didn't think I was good, pretty, or worthy enough of anyone's love. That love included my mother whom I adored. Being a kid in the early 70's, I desired to be loved all the time, only to receive the opposite. At the tender age of six, I was molested by an old white man while raking his grass. When I was seven: I was accidently set on fire while trying to light a cigarette for my mother and later knocked in the head by a clothesline pole while two girls swung on it. By the time I turned nine, I had been accidently locked in an old refrigerator while playing hide and seek, raped by my first husband at twenty, and rejected by men.

Why was I singled out? I used to wonder. Was it something about me that I had to be an example? Or was it because God knew I would be strong and overcome the pain? But was there *even* a God? Didn't He see what was happening to me? Did He even care? These were questions I had to ask myself because I sought God's love at an early age, and I knew He wouldn't allow this to happen to me.

When people asked me, "If you been through all this, how did you make it? Why aren't you angry instead of always smiling?

I'd smile and say, "BUT GOD!"

Silence…astonished faces flourishing the air.

"But God?" They would say.

"What does that even mean?"

"It means, if it weren't for God watching over me during these times, death would have swallowed me up."

Then one day, God spoke to me. "You are a living miracle. You have to do something to let my people know what I've done in your life." I couldn't believe what I was hearing. Was God speaking to me, or was it my mind flipping out on me? That was the day I knew God loved me. God had my back but did I have His? Did I always say or do what He commanded me to do? Seriously!

My head dropped in shame. I'm not perfect, and then I realized that God said in Ecclesiastes Chapter 7:20, "*For there is not just one man who does good And does not sin.* (NKJV). He couldn't find one. I smiled knowing God is always there for me and will forgive me for my sins whenever I seek Him through prayer.

One day while I was in bed, I heard another voice, "Are you ready? Can you handle it?"

I wanted so much to be ready. So, I said, "Yes Lord, I'm ready. I can do it!" But what was He referring? Can I handle… What? I was second guessing God. It was evident. I'm a writer and a playwright. Could I handle the pressure if one day I became famous? My answer was, "I'm not sure." To date, since I spoke those words, I have not yet been able to gain fame like my author counterparts. They've accepted the challenge and are doing well. They knew how to work the market and say the right things to keep them afloat. Sadly, I haven't because I've made excuses for everything, such as, I'm always too busy to engage in other things. "I'm just not ready," I told myself.

Then in 2010, I heard yet another voice, "You have to tell them. Write a book about your life and how you were able to survive the difficult times."

At first, I ignored what I heard because I just thought my mind was playing tricks on me. But then, two days later while at church, one of the ministers came up to me and said, "Donna, you write such good plays and books, why don't you write a book about your life and the trials and tribulations you've gone through?"

Then it was evident to me; I had to do this. But how? God gave me three months to write such a book, and at first,

I thought I had completed it. But then, more and more things started to happen, that I could not leave out! My memory of my life had gotten stronger. So, I decided to go somewhere where I could focus and write without interruption. I told my fiancé who is now my husband and he wanted to join me. I agreed. I didn't want to do this alone. I needed him with me. We ventured out, and here I am *six years later*. Had I listened back then; this novel would have been published but missing a lot of great moments.

Why I Write

Being a writer has brought many changes to my life. Sometimes living with the characters I've created. Portuguese has a feel of being promiscuous, fun-loving, and has a bountiful witty spirit. Donna, the name given to me at birth, is more like the religious soft spoken easy to get along with Lady.

Many times, in our lives we create an imaginary world outside our norm for different reasons. Mine stemmed from loneliness and needing attention. Being confined to a room as a child is depressing, devastating, and downright wrong. No one should ever have to be so lonely to where they create personalities just to please themselves.

I've cried many nights, hoping, praying, and searching for love when all along it was staring me right in the face. If only I'd put more faith in God and not in man, I'd still be married to my former husband. But who wants a man that's afraid to touch them, hold them, make love to them? No woman should ever deprive herself of being loved.

Though I've since found love again, at the time, I was in no hurry to commit myself wholeheartedly to a relationship without weighing my options. In fact, a mistake I made almost thirty years ago, almost repeated with the same man in 2009. I nearly gave into a man that I thought I still loved. But after meeting Terry who is my dear husband, I chose to have an enduring relationship with a man I knew would protect my heart and love me for the woman that I am.

I guess over the years, I have matured. The selfish part of me would have kept going to meet up with the other guy, but the God in me said, "No, he's had his opportunity and failed you many times." Our minds may tell us that we want something so bad, but our hearts will tell us what we truly need.

Nevertheless, when I first went looking for Donna Brown, I didn't know what or whom I would find. You see, Donna Brown was another name given to me by man. God gave me Donna Wright. Though there are some fictitious characters in my novel, many of them ring true in my life and in the lives of people I've encountered over the years.

Most people don't know this, but many individuals have split personalities, and if we are not careful, they can get you in trouble and can be hard to handle. Don't get me wrong;

I don't proclaim to have split or multiple personalities. I'm just saying that when we are born, we are born one way, but man can turn us into something we may not want to be. No one person has the same temperament every day, especially if you are in a relationship, work, or have kids.

Finding Me, Finding You, originally *Finding Me, The Donna Brown Story,* but God showed me something else on July 18, 2016, just a month before my 50th birthday. And Since I was no longer Donna Brown, I needed another title.

It's the real-life story of my dreams, life, and my pursuit of finding happiness again.

One day I looked in the mirror and said, "Girl, you look pathetic!" It was not my usual, "Girlfriend, you look good today!" In the past, I've told myself those words a thousand times, but then, I'd look inside myself and say, "You are a beautiful woman that God has created, and the devil is a liar." Often, searching for a way out but could not seem to find one. It could have stemmed from the way I felt about life at the moment, or maybe having the mind-frame of not being good enough to be loved by a decent man. At least, that's what my first husband always told me.

Daily, I would ask myself, "Who am I? And, why did God choose me to go through so many life changes?" With the many broken hearts and ailments stimulating from my first husband, I often wondered if I would see any more birthdays. At my lowest points in life, I seem to reminisce about past relationships shaking my head about accepting the way some men treated me. Wondering why? Could it have been the way they touched me or could it have been that my self-esteem was at its lowest point? But no matter what it was, I could never seem to shake the feeling of needing to be loved.

As I sat on my bed August 8, 2016, I sought pictures of my childhood trying to remember me as far back as I could. Wow! Those childhood memories! What would it be like to be that little girl again? Then I thought, "Hey, I don't want to be that kid anymore. That little girl was molested, raped, accidentally locked in a refrigerator, hit in the head with a steel clothesline pole, and left dejected by men." I want to be me—the lovely, passionate wife that God created me to be.

Finding Me, Finding You, will take you on a journey of my life and the life of others that you may be able to relate. For me to find me, I would have to search for the person that I used to be. I have created so many Alias for myself from the books that I have written, that often time, I find myself trying to live like them. I have finally decided to be who I am in God, rather than continually hide behind who I am not.

Here are key points I've set for myself to live life successfully:

- God. By placing God first in our lives, we will be able set our goals and accomplish our dreams.

- Family. God gave us a family so that we will be able to discover love and have a successful life.

- Love. Without love, you may never experience the pure joy of living. Be mindful that a kind heart gives us hope that one-day happiness will bring endurance to obtain

love for ourselves and those willing to receive it.

CHAPTER ONE

Who Am I?

Although I was born and raised as Donna Wright, one of my uncles David Wright gave me another name that has stuck with me for half a century, *'Portuguese.'* But, "Who is Donna Wright and where can I find her?" All my life I have lived for others doing what I thought would please them and trying not to hurt their feelings…but what about me? What do I want for myself? When will I be able to breathe? Shouldn't I be able to sit back, relax, and enjoy life for what it truly is? Not if I want to live life to its fullest extent.

My journey started years ago, as a child—always wanting to please others before myself, has left me shameful and despaired into my adult years. My life had taken such a toll on me that I didn't know who I was anymore. I was beginning to feel lost, lonely, and less desirable. I couldn't remember the last time I sought genuine love for myself.

When I decided to increase my moral stability, I also improved my ability to prosper. In 2009, I could find true happiness and profound joy in my life. Having the capacity to rediscover the person I was born to be, helped me reach a happy medium in life and do what Michael Jackson proclaimed in his song, "Off the Wall." I left all the things that brought unhappiness to my life and started to enjoy myself. That's when I realized that life wasn't so bad after all. Deciphering the words **Leave**, **Enjoy**, *and* **Life** equated to a much profound way of living for me.

- **Leave**—behind the misery and pain life has inflicted upon you.
- **Enjoy**—what God has created in your life—henceforth; family, friends, outdoors.
- **Life**—has a meaning of self-endurance, power, and existence beyond our belief.

When I left all the misery, pain, and suffering behind, I began to enjoy the life that God desired for me to have. For instance, as a child, I wanted desperately to grow up so that I could travel the world.

I saw a commercial, "it's not just a job… It's an adventure." A slogan the U.S. Navy has used for years to draw people in and it worked. I decided to join the Navy in 1988 and supposedly see the world. Ha, I didn't see the world for what I thought it would be like Paris, Rome, Africa, and Europe. But instead, I saw Iceland (cold, heartache, and pain), Maryland (Misery and suffering), and Georgia (Ignorance and prejudice).

Sometimes what we need in life takes precedence over what we want. For example:

When I was young, I was looking for someone to love because I didn't feel loved at home. This resulted in me growing up too fast. I started dating when I was fourteen and married six years later to the love of my life, *so I thought*. Instead of love and happiness, I found an act of violence and spousal rape. I was running faster than the Road Runner screaming, "Beep…Beep!" Once was good enough for me. But most women when in a situation like me tend to find excuses to stay:

- He said he wouldn't do it again.
- I provoked him.
- He didn't mean it.
- It was his first time.
- I have nowhere else to turn.
- But—I love him.

How many times have you said those exact words? I wouldn't allow myself even to think them because when I first married my ex-husband, I made three things clear to him if he ever put his hands on me:

1. I would burn the bed with him in it (From the movie, 'the Burning Bed');
2. I would tell my Uncle Raymond whom he was very afraid of; or
3. I would simply leave him.

He called me on all of them except me leaving. He completely forgot about it. When he said, "I guess you're going to burn the bed with me in it, huh?"

I fearfully said, "Don't be ridiculous; I bought that bed."

Then, he said, "Well, I guess you're going to call your uncle and rat me out!"

Again, out of fear for my life, I said, "C'mon, my uncle doesn't need to be bothered with my problems."

But before he could even suggest the last thing, I turned to him and said, "Besides, I *just told you* that I had slept with another man. I'm sure you didn't mean it."

But it was all a lie because from the moment we stepped foot at Fort Riley, Kansas, he kept asking me, "Who I was sleeping with?" I was livid at first that he would even ask such a question. Someone had placed it in his head, and he believed it.

He had no idea I was getting ready to leave him. I had five bags tightly packed to include my Oneida Silverware.

I wrapped them so tightly that not even a hearing aid could hear them rattling inside. I had to be smart, however. It was a matter of my life (telling him that I was leaving) or pretending to love him still and stay there for a couple more weeks until my flight took off. Then, I scurried around the apartment until I was able to get any and everything dear to me. I left and never looked back.

When we seek the undesirable, we find hardship in places less comforting than where we began. After hearing what I had gone through, an old friend of mine told me that, "We tend to settle for less because we can't have what we want." I wanted to be with him but was too afraid of being hurt again. So, how do you get what you want without losing sight of yourself?

First, of all:

- Seek the unknown, i.e., where you were before you lost control of yourself.

- Present yourself as a Lady.

- Dress casual and appropriate.

- Leave them wondering what your body looks like not the other way around.

- Don't give in on the first date; if he wants to be with you, he will be willing to wait.

- Destroy any negative feelings you have about yourself, i.e.,

    - Why can't I be built like so and so and such and such?

    - Maybe he won't like this about me.

The Death of Christopher Potter, my baby brother.
(Sunrise August 14, 1971 – Sunset March 29, 1972)

His smile was like fresh strawberries picked from a vine of purity. His skin—radiant to the touch. My eyes glistened every time I saw him. I was five, and he was newly born waiting for the world to capture his beauty. I fell in love with him from the time Mama walked through the old wooden screen door.

As time went on and days turn into months, I'd see myself tossing him high into the open air making him burst into laughter. All I could think was 'momma's going to kill me if I ever drop him.' Then it happened, a loud screeching sound coming from his mouth. It was enough to let me know that he was in great pain and I was in deep trouble. Mama dropped the dishtowel she was wiping her hands with and came running.

"What's wrong with him, Donna?"

If I had a quarter for the look on her face, I'd run up the sidewalk and buy a strawberry soda and a pack of lemon cookies.

His loud screeching scream turned into a slow wail. I gazed at Christopher. His saddened eyes told me that he was hot as fish grease!

"Augh, nothing Mama!" Christopher was in so much pain from hitting his head on the floor when I dropped him. I couldn't kiss the tears away fast enough! I had no idea how to ease his pain, and I felt utterly helpless. Christopher wouldn't let me touch him for weeks and when he did; his radiant smile glistened past his face. We must've played for hours until his beautiful little eyes began to close ever so slightly.

"Hi, Lil' man. You still love me?" his smiled beamed, and I knew he was okay. He finally dozed off, and I gently laid his soft body onto momma's bed.

Deep down inside, I knew Christopher did not understand one word I was saying, but he was such a happy baby filled with lots of joy. He had a smile that melted your heart like butter in a microwave.

The winter months were bitter for the first time; it seemed in Pensacola, Florida. We'd lived in Moreno Courts for nearly six years. Mama said we'd moved there after I was born. She had taken us away from where my grandmother lived when I was born and moved to New York with my aunt. She'd met this man, and when things didn't go well with him, she high tailed back to Pensacola and moved to Moreno Courts.

When Christopher was born, he was the sixth child momma had had in eight years. I was five at the time, and to me, he was my baby. But the winter of 1971 was brutal to Christopher's body, causing him to get extremely sick. His temperature was high, and he cried continuously.

Mama was young, and she had already had five children before she was twenty-five. Christopher was the extra special one that came after us. When Christopher's eyes turned into salty water, I knew something was wrong but couldn't figure it out. I remember standing there helpless not knowing what to do to make his tears go away. I tried everything to make him laugh, but it didn't happen.

Mama took him to Baptist Hospital in Pensacola, but they turned her away. They said he had a cold and it was nothing they could do.

I remember the anger momma felt when she left. How could a hospital turn an innocent baby away? So, she took him home but soon had to turn around. This time she took him to Sacred Heart Hospital where they discovered he had pneumonia.

They rushed him to the back and gave him sedation medicine before placing a trachea down his throat. But it was too late! Christopher's little heart couldn't take any more pain. I remember the scream that rang throughout the hospital from my momma's voice when the doctor said, "We did all we could. He's not suffering anymore."

Those were words momma did not want to hear. Her sixth child, Christopher Potter, was dead at seven months. When she came back without Christopher, I knew one or two things had happened. I'd never guessed in 1 million years that I'd never see my baby brother again. For years, I blamed myself because after all; I had dropped him. It wasn't until I became an adult that I was told differently; that he had pneumonia. I carried that burden until I was in my late twenties.

At Christopher's funeral, things didn't turn out so well. We were sitting with our heads down at Joe Morris Funeral Home when I got up to walk over to the casket, where he peacefully laid in his blue and white outfit.

"A baby?" I was so angry because I couldn't believe God had taken him away. My eyes flooded with tears as I reached inside the casket trying to lift his tiny little body that had become so heavy.

Mama was sitting with her brother Oscar Jones who we called Uncle Tin Top, her sister Claudell McGee, Uncle Raymond, and my stepfather John Potter, who we call 'June.' She jumped up so fast yelling for me to put that baby back in his casket.

His body was cold as ice, but that didn't stop me from trying to take him away again when momma busted me. I fell to the floor kicking and screaming. Mama finally took us away but not without me getting a last glimpse of my baby brother. How could I leave him there? He was going to be all alone. But I had no choice. He was dead, gone, and about to be buried.

I only remember a moment of his burial, but that was the one I'll always keep inside. His remains rest at the Good Hope Cemetery next to a tree in Warrington, Florida. Right next to him, rest his father, John William Potter. May they both rest in peace along with my mother, Annie Laura Wright, who is at the Rest Haven Cemetery.

CHAPTER TWO

Hide and Seek

The game of Hide and Seek can be so much fun especially when you hide in places that are hard to find. When you're a kid, the consequences of a good hiding place can turn into a nightmare. That's what happened to me, and it almost cost me my life.

Ever had items such as washers and dryers, refrigerators, old cabinets that have broken, and you placed them in your backyard because you had no way of getting rid of them? Well, back in the early 70s, we had an old white refrigerator with the raised handle that you had to lift and pull out to open the door. I remember that refrigerator so well because you see, I almost lost my life in it. It was hot and kind of late in the evening, and we wanted to play a game of Hide and Seek. I ran to the back of the house, and our neighbor, Ms. Clara Curry, was out in her garden cropping her seeds wearing her tan straw hat and overalls.

I thought I would be clever and hide in the refrigerator. I would only pull the door a little so it wouldn't shut tight. I waved at Ms. Clara and sssh'd her to silence. She stood watching me with a troubled look on her face. I didn't know why she had that look, but I soon found out.

My oldest sister Sharon and my brothers had found other places to hide. I could hear them coming so I closed the door a little more. Before I knew it, the latch caught and closed me in.

It was so dark inside. At first, I didn't know what to do, so I panicked. It got hot fast. I had on some tan shorts and a halter top that I feel helped me not to overheat. I started kicking and screaming, but no one came. They forgot all about me. I was all *alone*. Fear was in my heart. I knew I would die in that refrigerator that day. But God had other plans for me. He sent an angel my way. Somehow, when Ms. Clara noticed no one was playing Hide and Seek anymore, she remembered I was still in that refrigerator.

She had to walk around to the front of her house and through a small trail to reach me, because she had a chicken fence around her backyard so the kids wouldn't run through or step on her garden. My mom was with her.

When they found me, I had faded away and was passed completely out. Ms. Clara saved my life. Mama rushed me to the hospital, and they were able to revive me. After we had got back home, momma hurried and got rid of that old refrigerator. When I think about how close to death I was, I have no doubt that God has Angels on this Earth to protect us. I used to think I was a cat with nine lives because of all my near-death experiences. I should've been dead by now. But God and His infamous mercy saved my life repeatedly. And for that, I am eternally grateful, and will serve Him for the rest of my life.

Lesson Learned:

- If you have old appliances in your backyard, discard them immediately. Don't let your child be a statistic like I almost was.

- Keep a close eye on your children and know where they are always.

- Never let your small children go unnoticed for more than two seconds. If by chance they come up missing:

- Call out to them.
  - Never stop looking for them.
  - Always keep a lock on appliances and cabinets you wish to disregard.

Being Free

Now that your eyes have completely watered with tears, let's clear our minds and focus on what this book is all about. Imagine yourself being free from the troubles that bog you down daily, i.e., —stress, jealousy, confusion, men. Now, imagine yourself—in a world where fantasies turn into dreams and dreams into reality.

Let me take you on a journey where fantasies, self-help, dreams, and reality encountered my world. Then—stress, confusion, divorce, and loneliness turned my life into a living disaster, until God intervened and gave me a new outlook on life. I wanted to start this one off on a positive note. However, I decided to put fiction into my opening and teaching into your life. I think this one will be something most of us can relate to at some point in our lives whether you're male or female.

Before I go into the teaching aspect of this book, I would like to give you a little taste of my writing world with a snazzy bit of romance.

There's a saying that a cat has 'nine lives.' But what if that saying was for a human—say like a lady Leo—a Lioness? A part of me believes that God gave me 'nine lives' because when I look at my life and see all the tragedies that have taken place, all I can say is "Thank You, Lord, for all You've done for me." Whether it was a clothesline pole busting my head open, being locked in a refrigerator in the middle of summer, or having a mild stroke in Keflavik, Iceland at 23, my lifeline seems to be without number. Each incident led me to be unconscious and seeing people in the bright light.

Sit back, relax, and enjoy. Some of this will contain things that might make you want to go out and kick someone. Then, there will be times when you can just laugh about it. So, let's have some fun.

CHAPTER THREE

The Day My Life Ended

Ladies and gentlemen,

Life is short and tomorrow may never come. So why do we stress over things we can't control? Did you know there is a "Silent Killer" waiting to take you out of this world? It's called, "High Blood Pressure." It can come from many different things such as:

- Stress
- Overweight
- Poor Diet
- Depression
- Tobacco
- Excessive Alcohol

When you go to the doctor, and they take your blood pressure; basically, they are looking for two common factors:

- Systolic—the force of blood moving through your arteries as the heart beats.
- Diastolic—the force of blood moving through your arteries as the heart rests.

According to the Centers for Disease Control and Prevention, approximately one in five individuals has the illness and is unaware. High blood pressure affects more than 67 million American adults thus increasing their risk of heart disease and stroke. It's the leading cause of death in the United States.

I remember back in January 1990, at the age of twenty-three, I had a rude awakening while serving my country in Keflavík. I was getting ready for work and went into the community shower down the hall from my room.

After turning the shower on and undressing, I stepped in. A weird sensation went through my arms, and I thought someone was playing a nasty joke on me. So, I yelled out, "Hello, this ain't funny!" But no one was there. 'Odd,' I thought to myself. So, I stepped back into the shower a second time, and the pain got worse. Now I was upset because this was the sickest joke anyone could play on me. Again, I stepped out and yelled, "C'mon on ladies! I have to get ready for work. The jokes over."

But when I stepped back inside, my hands locked, my mouth twisted, and I started losing consciousness. Someone walked into the bathroom in time for me to yell out, "Get my roommate!" It was the last words I uttered for a few hours.

There I was, a twenty-three-year-old one hundred fifteen-pound young lady having a mild stroke. I wasn't overweight, didn't drink or smoke, but that didn't stop me from stressing out and being depressed in such a cold place; almost losing my life. My grandmother, the only grandparent I've ever known, had passed in October 1990, and there I was on the verge of joining her three months later.

I don't remember much about the incident other than my cousin Mary Harris telling me that a Navy Chief had brought me downstairs after they dressed me. Someone had placed me on the floor next to the front door of the barracks where it was freezing outside. The temperature had fallen to minus 18° with nearly three feet of snow. The worse part about it was that the ambulance couldn't get close enough to the door to take me to the hospital, because the snow hadn't been shoveled.

It took them nearly two hours to shovel a path so that the paramedics could roll me out the door. Meanwhile, my life was drifting slowly away. That's how I knew there was a God and He was watching over me that night. I could have easily been banished from the Earth and never had a family. But God kept me here because He knew my two sons had to be born, and I was the vessel that He had chosen to give birth to them.

When people talk about seeing people in white waving and smiling at them while they are unconscious, it's the God's given truth. My God! I had seen so many people in that bright light, and here I am once again to tell how God spared my life and made me a living testimony.

After they finally cleared the path, my cousin Mary said that as I was lying on the floor saying, "Okay, all right, all right." Then, I would black out again. I have no idea what that meant, but I do know when they took me outside uncovered, I shook for a few seconds. I only had on a pair of gray sweats and a gray cut off Florida A&M University sweatshirt. They didn't even put socks on my feet.

After they finally cleared the snow, they rushed me to a local hospital on base. I woke up remembering it being the smallest hospital I've ever seen, and a doctor by the name of Knickels saying, "Welcome back." I saw all the bright lights and looked at him and asked, "Welcome back? From where?"

He chuckled replying with a huge smile, "You were out for over three hours. We thought we'd lost you. We believe that you had a mild stroke."

Those words resonate through my soul until this day. You see, every time I get a sharp chest pain, twitching in my lips, burning or numbness on my left side of my body, I pause because I am reminded of how close I was to death. I'm not overweight, not a heavy drinker, and I don't smoke. But I still stress over things I cannot change, like my mom's death back in January 2002 or my husband's near death on January 27, 2016.

Amazing, isn't it? I almost lost my life on January 1, 1990, and twelve years later, on January 12, 2002, my mother passed having a stroke, heart attack, and an aneurysm. Hypertension is real, and until we take control of our lives, it can take control resulting in premature death.

I realized that for me to remain on this side of the Earth, I had to be alert—knowing every inch of my body, be aware of what was going on around me and stay focused on what mattered to me. It is imperative to also know the signs of a stroke (tingles, dizziness, numbness).

If you have any of the symptoms, please don't hesitate. Call 911 without procrastinating. Knowing that hypertension, stroke, or a heart attack has no age limit and can strike at any time, I take notice to any pain my body tells me, and I head to the emergency room right away.

Another important factor in this situation is to know the medications you are on. Some of the medicines that my doctors prescribed have led to the conditions I've suffered.

CHAPTER FOUR

Confessions

S ome say, "Confession is good for the soul," but what is a conscience without redemption? Confess your sins and all will be well with thee. True, but not so true. Say, for instance, you pour out your heart to someone, and you really didn't mean to let out all your secrets or ghosts (as some would say). What will that person think of you now? Will they look upon you with the same respect? Will they forgive you if they were the person you hurt? You must take into consideration that all of us are not of the same mind and body in Christ. Just because we finally decided to let go of our frustrations, anger, and secrets, does not mean everyone will be as accepting as the next. What are some of the confessions you hold that may be blocking your blessings?

- **The boss**—So you've been eyeing your boss for the past couple months. You knew he had lost his wife and his family in a house fire and now you're thinking, *He's* *got to be lonely. I'll just ease my way into his life, and he won't know what hit him.*

- **The spouse**—I'm so tired of this lazy man. He doesn't do anything but lay around all day long and expect dinner on the table when he comes home from work. Sometimes, I wish he'd just go away.

- **Your best friend's husband**—"Curtis sho 'nuff' been keeping himself in shape." You think to yourself, *just as soon as Nicky turns her back, Curtis will be mine. I'm a good-looking woman, and I know I got great sex appeal. Maybe if I smile extra hard, he'll like me too.*

Okay ladies, how many of these situations have you been in lately or in the past? Don't lie to yourself! I can honestly say that I have engaged in one of them in my lifetime. God sends me a reminder every now and then to let me know that I must confess my sins and He will be gracious enough to forgive me. Whether they be sins of omission or commission, life and death are in the power of the tongue. What we say from our mouth can never be taken back. Be careful how you express your confessions. Once the words are out, even if you don't mean to say them that way, you can never take them back.

For example:

I was in a deep conversation with my ex-husband years ago, and I was concerned about him lying around all the time. I walked into our room while he was lying down and said, "Look, don't take this the wrong way, but you're going to die on your side if you don't stay off it."

His retaliation back to me was brutal. I had to admit, I was crushed. So, I got angry, and my response was even worse. Sometimes, we have to watch what we say to those we love the most and try and work things out, so that no one's feelings will be hurt.

So, why do we use words to hurt those we proclaim to love? Sometimes, words can be so damaging that you can't find your way back to one another.

When we finally decide to confess our wrong doings, are we confessing to the significant other or are we confessing to God? Many times, what we think is a confession is a tale of made up lies. I made a mistake over twenty-two years ago, (November 1987) of telling my first ex-husband what I thought he wanted to hear. He had this thing called, "Confession Friday." It was supposed to be where we told each other if another male or female tried to come on to us or even spoke to us during the week. It was his idea and his way of controlling me. The funny part about it was, I was doing all the confessing. He never seemed to have anything to confess about.

After a couple of cold months in January 1988, I decided enough was enough and I wasn't going to take his mess anymore. I packed all that I could and never looked back.

Yeah, confession is good for the soul. But sometimes, it's just best to confess to God and ask Him to forgive you of your sin. Some men will never understand why you do the things you do. But God already knows what you're going to do before you do it. You should always clear your mind with a counselor or God, not someone who constantly judges you.

Chapter Five

Inner Relationship Rape

November 1987 . . . Fort Riley Kansas

Imagine! Being woken up in the middle of the night to what you thought would be a great night of bonding. Now, imagine your clothes being ripped off and you being told by your spouse, "I bet I could make you do anything right now." It could happen. It did happen. In 1981, I dated a young man for over six years before we got married. I thought I was on top of the world. I was only fourteen when I fell in love with him. We did everything together. But one thing I never thought would happen in a million years was the love of my life would rape me.

After we had dated for a few months, he was given orders to go to Germany. Throughout my whole high school years, I missed out on proms, dances, and other important events that young girls should enjoy while in school.

But I was dating a senior, and no other girl knew what it felt like as a freshman to have a man. At least, that's what I thought. So, when he had teased me a few times about getting married and then turning around saying, "Sike," I was furious. I decided to call him on it one day. I purposely said, "Hey, let's get married."

He replied, "Okay."

And before He knew it, I was running through the house telling everyone that I was getting married. *Be very careful what you ask for.* He was appalled. He didn't think I was serious until I called my aunt and uncle. Then, it sunk in. He was going to be a married man. That would ruin his reputation with the women, though.

After we had got married in August of 1986, things went downhill. Had I known back then what I know now, he would have been a distant fantasy that never came true. It all started with us preparing to move to Fort Riley, Kansas. The day started off with an awful vibe. He had left to say his goodbyes to his family, and I stayed behind. Across the street from where we lived, was the man I had fallen in love within just a few months while my husband was away in basic training. And now, I had to leave Al behind.

In my mind, He couldn't get up and go fast enough. Before I knew it, I quickly ran across the street trying to rekindle the last bit of loving, Al and I shared. Al did things for me that He couldn't imagine doing. I knew I was wrong, but my ex-husband has called and told me that he had shared a dinner with another female. I couldn't believe he'd do that to me.

I got back just in time to make it look like I'd been moving, packing, and working hard. When my husband walked in the door five minutes later, I was sweating like crazy. To walk away from him was the worst and the best thing I could have ever done.

Then we had to leave. Leaving my mother behind literally broke my heart. But even worst, leaving Al crushed my soul. We arrived at Fort Riley, Kansas already in turmoil. The entire ride was devastating. I wanted to drive that U-Haul off a cliff from the torture my husband had put me through. He always hounded me about who I was sleeping with. I didn't understand at first. Then it made sense. Someone had told him about Al coming to the apartment while he was away. *Be real careful who you call a friend, because they will stab you in the back faster than you can blink an eye.* The only person that could have told him was the guy who lived below us. I saw him talking to him from my window as I was packing. I just didn't know what they were talking about.

For three months, he accused and pestered me about who I was sleeping with. Then, I remember him telling my mother that he was going to mistreat me when we got to

Kansas. Things were slowly falling out of control, fast. So, I finally created a story. I thought he would call me on it. (*Again, from the previous situation, you should only confess to a Counselor or to Christ*).

I made up a story about a guy named James that used to work with me at the Post Exchange. I just knew he would call me on it. He called me on it alright. He jumped up eyes raging with fury screaming at me, "You have to go!" His eyes were so demonic they would have scared the devil himself.

So, I thought I'd be smart and say, "I'm going." Then I did the stupidest thing ever. I went to our room and laid on the bed. He came after me and started choking me and pulling my hair. *God, I thought I was going to die right then and there!*

After realizing what he'd done, he jumped up and said, "I guess you're going to burn the bed with me in it?" I had to be smart in my reply because I had previously told him if he put his hands on me, I would do just that!

So, I said, "No, I'm sure you were hurt hearing that I slept with someone else." Not that I hadn't, because I had been with Al. 'Yes, I was young, foolish, and naïve.

So, was I wrong seeking love in all the wrong places? Maybe. Maybe not. Two nights later, I found myself in another situation I couldn't get out of. The clock on the nightstand flashed 12:02 a.m. Next thing I knew, he jumped from his sleep like a wild man tearing my clothes off. He looked at me with a slight smirk on his face and said, "I bet I can make you do anything right now." I was scared to death.

My only reply was, "huh?"

After he had raped me, he looked down at me again and pushed me aside. The words he uttered next have lingered in my ears until now. Calling me outside my name really hurt coming from him. I laid still with tears flowing down my cheeks. I didn't make a sound because I was afraid of what he might do.

Later that morning, he fixed his mouth to say, "And what's wrong with you?"

"You don't remember what you did to me?" I came back at him. "You ripped my clothes off me, and you raped me. How could you do that to me?" I said tearfully,

He dropped his head and said, "I thought I was dreaming."

"You're lying, and you know it. When you jumped me a couple days ago and offered to take me to the hospital after hurting me, I should have taken you up on that offer."

"I'm sorry," was all he could say.

Knowing what I know now, had I gone to the hospital and told someone what he did to me, I probably wouldn't have suffered the humiliation of being raped by my own husband.

Sometimes, I catch myself being too honest with my dear husband. I tell him everything from past relationships to men proposing to me at the store, to an old boyfriend that seems to resurrect from my past after twenty years…Al.

If you're in a situation where you've been raped or feel threatened by the person that you're with, get as far away from the person as possible. The life you save could renew the destiny and self-esteem you have left inside.

When my ex-husband grabbed me by the hair yanking me backward on November 1, 1987, and raped me on November 3, 1987, I thought it would be the end of me. I just knew that he was going to kill me. But he got up and began shouting, "You gotta go! You gotta go!" It was as if the Satan himself was speaking through him with a strong desire to finish what he'd started! But something got a hold of him, and he ran towards the living room and called his father. Had I not been screaming to the top of my lungs, I probably wouldn't be sitting here typing this today. I sighed hard because I know it could have been much worse. I was truly defenseless when it came to him. I'd never let anyone get the best of me, but He did.

Over the years, I've learned that complete disclosure is not always the best policy, especially when it comes to relationships, nor is making up imaginary affairs. Some things are better kept between you and your Maker. Ask God for forgiveness instead of telling a deranged spouse that you've done something unthinkable.

The fact of the matter is that some men think it's okay if they are out having fun with other women, but as soon as the fear of their woman being with another man encounters their minds, rage takes over! Remember this: Unspoken words are much better than words spoken when it comes to life-or-death situations. Speaking the truth may cost you your life depending on the situation.

I've learned to be true to myself and ask God for forgiveness rather than expecting forgiveness from mere humans.

Low Self-Esteem

To this day, I often tell myself, "I'm not pretty enough, too fat, or he's not attracted to me because I don't look as good as Janet Jackson, Mariah Carey, or Halle Berry?

I was born pigeon-toed, developed crooked teeth with a gap, and developed stretch marks and varicose veins while serving my country. Since the beginning of my life, I dealt with the embarrassment of being ridiculed because my feet were crooked, and I had a slight bow in my legs. Let alone, I was so skinny. I practically made Olive Oyl look fat. Guys laughed at me. The girls turned their noses up because I had appeal but not the body. I was so embarrassed that I would be afraid to walk in front of people.

I thought maybe one day that I would grow out of my imperfections and get over my fears of walking in front of individuals. Trying to correct the way I walk or cover my mouth got old. Most people probably wouldn't notice if I didn't bring attention to myself. If my mother could have fixed these two things while I was little, it would have made all the difference in the way I see myself today. But she couldn't afford to have them repaired. We were poor, but we didn't know it. Momma made sure of that.

I used to feel like there were problems with my body that hindered me from getting that special someone. Most of the time, I kept my head down because guys used to call me, 'Barbie.' These, and many other flaws made me feel like I wasn't worthy to have a decent man in my life. I had severe problems with low self-esteem, but then I asked myself these simple questions:

- Am I blind, crippled, or deaf?

- Does my skin suffer from extreme eczema?

- Is my skin burnt to the point where I'm unrecognizable?

- Do I have all my teeth, arms, and legs?

Since I couldn't answer these questions with a simple "no" then what was I complaining about? When I look in the mirror and see the person looking back at me, sometimes I smile and say, "You don't look so bad." After all, God could have made me the same way He made those other people. God made us a certain way because He knew that if we were made to be other than how we are, we wouldn't be able to handle it.

I can only imagine how someone born blind, crippled, or deaf may feel about the way they were created. We should never feel bad about the way God created us because He created us in His image.

I had to find something within myself that would build my confidence level and build my self-esteem to a satisfactory degree. Instead of putting myself down, I decided to take a deep long soothing breath and exhale slowly. I went to the mirror and said to myself, "Life ain't so bad after all."

Then, I thought about the person that couldn't look in the mirror and smiled. I have eyes to see, legs to walk, and ears to hear. I had to remind myself that someone out there was in worse shape than me. But through the grace of God, I knew I would make it.

When I decided to begin recognizing my value, I felt better about myself.

For instance:

When my first ex-husband used to tear me down, I thought I was the ugliest person on Earth. Countless days, I would hear, "No man would ever want you because you're too skinny and you're not pretty." I used to believe this for years until I met my second husband, and many other males wishing they had what my husband had. My ex-husband didn't appreciate until I was gone.

At this point in my life, I've learned to look in the mirror and say, "You are a beautiful black woman, and any man would be proud to call you, his wife."

When I find myself drifting back into depression, my husband always seems to sense what I am going through. I'll either receive an email, call, or text message saying, "Hello Sweet Cheeks, thought I'd reach out to you to see how you were doing." I once heard a Radio Announcer on 96.3 FM in Augusta, Georgia, say, *"When you have a man that makes you feel like a million bucks, you won't let nothing or no one tear you down."* Thank God, after the drama was over, we found the love we both were searching for. Now, that I found love again, the way I feel about myself has changed, and my self-esteem has increased.

~

Build up your confidence! Don't let nothing or no one tear you down. We're all beautiful in God's eyes. Take yourself to a movie or even to dinner. Put on your best dress, and leave that nine to five upon the shelf, and just enjoy yourself… just like the late Michael Jackson said.

~

I love my husband for that, because he knew what I was going through instead of taking advantage of me, he would always give me advice, be a dear friend, and watch over me.

Depression
Summer 2009

I've cried, but I don't know why. I've walked around in circles and yet, I've cried some more. The hot streaming tears embraced my red-hot face, and yet, I don't know why.

My lips are trembling, and my hands are shaking wondering if it's Vertigo; or am I just a baby? Why am I walking around without a care in the world knowing I have two boys, a family, and a dog? Yet, I stay confined in my room—a room I created for me by me. My world—the world where Panama, Japan, and Germany all meet the four corners of the walls I've designed for me to live in. From dolls to scrolls to Alpaca rugs hanging over my bed, over my futon—a place where I hide from the rest of the world—from my family.

Why am I hiding from a life that I created over twenty years ago? I cry silently within myself asking God, "why?"

When I find myself continuously crying, I ask the question, "What's wrong with you girl?" I finally came to a conclusion, that I was suffering from *Depression*, a severe disease that if not taken care of properly can lead to death. For years, I've experienced chest pains and migraine headaches, and I had no idea why I was getting them so frequently.

As I sought one physician after another rushing from emergency rooms both in Maryland and Georgia, I'd wonder why I had such sharp pains in my chest and a burning sensation on my left side. It could have been a heart attack or stroke threatening if I wasn't careful.

But in reality, I had suffered a mild stroke, anxiety, depression, and panic attacks since January 1990 while serving my country.

"Wow," I thought. At such a young age, too. What was it that made my chest pound so hard taking every breath I breathe away and leaving me breathless? Was I that unhappy with my life? Were the pressures of this world closing in on me?

Given the many opportunities in life, I've chosen to take a road traveled by many instead of the road less traveled.

The author, Robert Frost wrote a poem, *The Road Not Taken*, that begins with:

Two roads diverged in a yellow wood,
And sorry I could not travel both…etc.

Many roads are meant to be taken, but only one can be taken at a time. Depression can be a lonely road filled with stress, deceit, and death.

What are some causes of depression?

- **The loss of a loved one**—no one handles death the same. Some people accept death and move on but with most people, death can be detrimental and leave a huge hole in your heart: i.e., loss of parent, child, or spouse.

- **Economy**—If you're like many that have been saving for your retirement and with the recent (2008 – 2009) fall of the stock market, you woke up one morning and found that most of your 401K or pension funds were depleted … This more than likely caused you to go into an economic depression.

- **Separation/Divorce**—Imagine being told after twenty years of marriage and the frequent, *I love you(s)* "I can't do this anymore. I want my freedom." Not only will it leave you emotionally torn, but in a state of depression. You are left trying to pick up the pieces, wondering how you're going to make it without your spouse.

- **Weight Gain**—Will he still love me now that I no longer have a supermodel figure? Having kids can place unwanted weight on us that may be hard to get rid of. No matter how hard you try, chocolate ice cream and cookies late at night can't seem to leave you alone.

Remember, you are not alone. Millions of women and men face depression daily. Remove yourself from the situation. Try going to the movies, getting a favorite book, treating yourself to the spa, or even a weekend getaway.

When the pressures of life tend to weigh me down, I book a flight to Florida. I would go and see my family, or even sometimes, I'd go on a trip created in my mind just for me. That trip could be on an island with no one there but the sound of waves rolling in and out of the sea. I'd see the beautiful ships sailing by and wonder where on Earth they could be going. I'd watch the birds flying over my head and ask, "Could I fly away with you?"

Once, I took a trip to Baltimore where I and several of my friends got together at a place called *Jaspers*. It was the most refreshing time I've had in a long time. Sometimes when I remove myself from a situation, I come back refreshed and renewed.

We may never know the exact causes of depression, but I've learned over the years that medication only made it worse for me. The last thing you need is to become addicted to *Paxil*, or one of the other drugs intended for depression. I found when taking one of the commonly known depressants, I'd cry more. My lips would tremble, and my mind would slow down. I removed myself from those drugs and became dependent upon prayer. If we allow Christ to enter our minds and our hearts more often, the troubles that we seem to go through decreases and the beauty of life shines through us.

CHAPTER SIX

Letting Go

When I decided to let go and let God handle my problems, I found peace and comfort. Although it was a struggle over the years, I finally came to the realization that after nine long years of being in a room secluded from my family, that it was time to break free and let misery take comfort elsewhere.

I fought demons of economic oppression, low self-esteem, and being a victim of circumstance far too long. But how does one break away from years of laughter, love, and devotion to years of agony, loneliness, and desertion?

- **Prayer**—it changes things. For years, I've prayed, "Lord help me make the right decision by putting you first, family second, and everything else last." In reality, everyone else came first, God second, and my family last. However, I've always placed my kids above myself.

- **Ambition**—you must have the drive and be willing to see the writing on the wall. When you make the decision to leave or stay, you have to be able to stick with it and live with the decision you've made. Not always second guessing yourself.

- **Persevere**—Do the unthinkable. Dream like never before. You could never get ahead of the game if you don't put forth the effort and try. Make time to grasp life. Set goals and stick to them.

For instance: I've been writing romance novels, Gospel plays, and children's books since 2001. But I never had the drive to take them past Augusta, Georgia, out of fear of being laughed at; or not enough commitment from the team players. I have a garage full of books that should be in the hearts of children or in the hands of women sipping on a tall glass of sweet tea or a tasty glass of red wine.

When you set forth your goals and follow them, only great things will come from it.

So, let's look at commitment and the married woman. Have we allowed ourselves to be fully committed to our husbands, or are we half stepping until the "so-called" perfect person walks through the door?

What is commitment anyway? According to Webster's Dictionary, a commitment is an obligation, a pledge or a promise. Basically, giving yourself to someone totally without rhyme or reason. When we break that bond, we let go of trust, love, and honesty. So, are women to blame for our lack of commitment in marriage/relationship? Not necessarily. Men are also responsible. Because of their lack of enthusiasm or staying out late portraying their doggish ways, many women have lost faith in men altogether when it comes to a family.

For years, commitment lay in the thought that women were too scared to pursue a relationship outside the marriage because the fear of being caught, embarrassment to the family, and the husband finding out.

However, women have ventured out and discovered that not only men but more women have someone on the side. Women have a unique way of hiding what they don't want to be known. For years, a girlfriend of mine had concealed a relationship that she was having with a married man. Her husband knew nothing about it.

According to her, when she was fed up with what her husband was doing, she started to step out and do what he was doing. Of course, she was called outside of her name because women aren't supposed to do what men get away with.

So, why are women called names but it seems okay for men to do the same thing?

I'll tell you why. Many males in my opinion are weak, because women can play the same game they are playing and without being caught. That only shows that women not only know how to get away with cheating, but also know how to keep their composure when they are around their significant other.

When my girlfriend decided to *step out*, she was tired of the late-night stories he would conjure up: "Baby, I had to work late" or "I stopped by my partner's house for a beer." She had a family, a house *(not a home)* because a home is shared by everyone and not just one. She had a good job, but after she had realized she could do bad all by herself, she decided to leave the pain of being married to the wrong man *(some twelve years)* behind and enjoy herself. My friend is now fifty-two years old, single, and has a big house to call her own.

She decided to let go of the pain, unwanted heartache, and deception of a cheating husband. She was willing to let go and step out on faith. Maybe letting go and finding herself was the best thing that happened to her in years.

Some of the ways she found faith in her broken relationship were:

- **Prayer**—Many times, we do things without praying. Then, we wonder why our lives fell apart so quickly. Say a simple prayer, find a verse in the Bible, live by it daily, and watch God change your life, and/or situation for the better.

- **Counseling**—When *she decided* that she needed more than prayer, she tried counseling. For years she prayed,

"Dear God, my life is spinning out of control," she wanted to fix her relationship with her ex-husband.

Unlike my friend, I gave up on my marriage because in my praying to God, instead of getting a quick fix, I kept seeing the wrong in him. His lack of interest, not helping around the house, being a bed potato instead of couch potato, encouraged me to leave my household and find peace. I didn't seek a counselor after many years. I chose to let go of twenty-one years of togetherness for what I saw as freedom.

My ex-husband once told me in October 2009, "You may think the grass is greener on the other side." What he didn't realize is that the grass was greener, and it was a pasture.

Those words have since stuck in my mind. However, I still chose to leave my life with him behind. I had no idea where this so call *freedom* was going to lead, but I knew I won't be stuck in a small bedroom being lonely anymore. Then, I exhaled. By exhaling, I took a deep soothing breath, held it in, and slowly released the agony I had been experiencing for over ten years.

Wow! I'd finally done it. I let go of a bad situation and was living my life the way I wanted to live it. Not how a man wanted me to live it. For years, I tried exhaling. But after celebrating my forty-third birthday in August 2009, I was able to breathe normally.

Although I left it all behind, a part of me will always remain in his life because we have two wonderful boys together, and the love that we shared as a family will never end. So, now that I've gone through these necessary steps of letting go, I feel rejuvenated. I really do! I feel like I have let go of years of stress, depression, and pain. Now, I am heading in a new direction.

I hope that I have said something here that will inspire you to make the necessary choices you need to help you get on with your life and be found by the person that you've been searching for, for years.

CHAPTER SEVEN

Finding Love Again

Over the years, I have read several novels trying to find joy in the words others had to offer. They led me to start writing books of my own. Now, that these words have come to past in my novels, I realize my God given talent is to help women find themselves and discover how powerful their minds could be.

Many people take romance for granted. They grow sour on love, tense up on a kiss, and pitty-pat when hugged. But what is true love? Some would say it's the joy of seeing that special someone walking through the door every day. Others may say, it's the passion felt when they're kissed on the nape of their neck, on the ears, or on the lips. But for me, it's the look in his eyes when he wants to play. Seeing his dark-skinned body moving towards me makes my body pause and my eyes glisten. Other times, it's upon hearing his voice, *"Hello Mrs. Hodges,"* whispering in my ear every time the phone rings or he sees me. Whatever it is, you must allow your mate the space to interact with you intimately.

There are times when the phrase *'action speaks louder than words,'* comforts me when I really want to know how he feels about me. Now, I know many people seek love and passion daily, but are we giving it back? Do you feel like he expects too much because you just had his child or been working all day cooking, cleaning, washing, and can't seem to keep up? Or being a man, do you feel her expectations of you coming home from a hard day's work is warranted by a simple kiss? Well, somehow you need to figure out how to adjust your time so that you will be able to handle your business.

Imagine this! One day you're coming home from work, and you walk through the door, and all you see is emptiness. Yeah, your place is filled with furniture and all the fixings but your heart is empty, lonely, and suffering from a lack of romance. Now *imagine…*walking through that same door knowing that every time you turn over at night that the love of your life is on the other side of the pillow waiting to embrace your warm arms and meet your every need. Ask yourself this, would you much rather come home to comfort, love, and romance, or loneliness, stress, and lots of mechanics? Feeling love is potential but being loved is essential. I say this because I used to be in loveless situation. I prayed for years asking God to remove me from the man that couldn't seem to find a way to love me. It took ten years but I stepped out on faith, and by doing so I ran into the man that had enough love planted inside his heart to share with a lonely woman like me.

If we forget as individuals the spark that kindled the flame in the first place, then someday someone may walk up to you and say, *Excuse Me, But I'm in Love with Your Husband or Wife*, also the title of my third book. The woman in this book took her husband for granted. She let herself go—because she had the *'I already have him'*, attitude. She forgot that the house needed cleaning, the clothes needed washing, and the man needed to be loved.

A not so good friend of mine enlightened me years ago, about love when I was sixteen. She told me, "Donna, I know you love him, but one day someone is going to come along and tear you guys apart." I had no idea she was talking about herself. That day opened many avenues in my life. I learned how to love, why to love, and when to love.

I've also learned that men like peace in their homes. No man wants to come home, and you're always nagging him. He wants to be held and told how much he really means to you. Men are like newborn babies. You have to pamper them all the time. If his shoulders need rubbing, by all means rub them.

I'm thinking back to when my dear husbands' feet were hurting so bad, and he asked me to rub them. Now, my husband doesn't have the best-looking feet in the world, but they were his feet—a part of us. I believe the whole man comes with the package of being married. You can't just put the ring on and be done with him. You must be there when he needs you the most.

Ladies, you will know when your man is happy because his eyes will tell the story. When I look in my husband's eyes, they seem to smile back at me. There's a lot of love that I believe he didn't have before he met me. Besides, his own daughter told me one time, "My daddy must really love you because I've never seen him laugh this much since I was a little girl." She is now twenty-four, and his eyes are still smiling at me.

Take the time to show your spouse how much you love them, and in the end, their eyes will smile back at you. Remember this: Love sometimes knocks at your door one time. If that is the time you decide to show off, love may never knock again.

Deception

Deception in my terms is an act of deceiving a person of goods or intentional lying to cover up a mishap without being caught. One of the most common errors that are made in a relationship is deception. When you meet someone for the first time, many times you trust what they are saying to be true. But, too often, a person will lie to cover up who they really are.

Some of the more common things a man or woman will lie about to gain your trust are:

- **Who they are**—their name, where they live, even gender, which could easily be determined after they reveal themselves to you.

- **Relationship**—how many different women they had in their lives. If there are current partners, do they or have they ever had any diseases such as Herpes, Gonorrhea, or VD.

- **Finances**—many times a person will build themselves up to be something they aren't, i.e., trying to live like the Jones's to sustain dignity, win you over, or even to gain friendship with a person of a higher standard.

- **Faithfulness**—In a relationship, honesty, integrity, and trustworthiness are key elements to maintaining a healthy relationship. Men and women have a hard time letting go of the past i.e. *(an old boyfriend or girlfriend),* so they tend to keep them in the closet just in case a fight or breakup occurs within their current relationship.

Remember: Honesty is the best policy. Just be honest.

CHAPTER EIGHT

Things Your Mother Should've Taught You But Didn't

You see, as a child growing up, I wanted to know the what's, when's, how's, and why's in life. Yes, I played outside and hung out with my friends often. However, on Saturdays, I would be at church cooking with my mother and some of the other *Willing Workers*. By the time I was eight years old, I was cooking full course meals, and my family enjoyed it so much that my mother would allow me to cook when I came home from school.

But times have changed and so have women. These days, women have forgotten their responsibilities to their daughters because their mothers forgot to train them. Their moms are so busy going out to the clubs, that they forget they have children left behind trying to fend for themselves. They don't make time to train their daughters, because most of them had daughters when they were teenagers. Yes, that's right.

Many girls don't become successful women because their mothers didn't have time to stay at home and nurture them.

Here are some things I think their moms should have taught the…because apparently, they don't know. I remember my mother telling me these three things about keeping the home front clean:

Three reasons you should always clean behind yourself:

1. So, that you will be able to get a husband one day.
2. So, that you don't give off an unpleasant odor.
3. Because it's ethical.

When should you clean behind yourself?

1. Every day if need be. You never know when someone will show up at your house.
2. Often. By cleaning often, things won't build up, and you won't keep putting it off until the end of the week.

For some people, this is true but for the most part, women more so than men have forgotten what these words mean. For instance, let's look at cleanliness. How many houses have you recently visited and the first thing a woman says is, "Please excuse the mess. I wasn't expecting anyone to come over."

Didn't expect company? Come on ladies, your house especially the living room area and kitchen should never bring you to the point where you have to apologize for it being nasty.

I remember growing up feeling like the Cinderella of our home. I got up at dust and made sure our house was spic and span. My mother never had to apologize for having a dirty house because she had me.

I often wonder if other girls were taught to cook and clean as I was. I never really asked questions when it came to cooking or cleaning, I just watched my mother and others and went from there. I often praise God for my Aunt Mable and Uncle Raymond who took me under their wings at sixteen and showing me how to become a Lady. Proverbs 22:6 says, "Train up a child in a way he should go and when he is old, he will not depart from it."

Wow! How powerful is that?

In becoming a woman, first, you must put aside, "girlish ways and present yourself as a woman." That means… Raising children and not exposing your body so that the entire world can see it. More so than ever, women are the biggest influence young ladies have today. It is very shameful, in my opinion, once a woman starts to have children or hit the age of twenty-one to lack cleanliness. It should've already been instilled in her how to conduct herself.

Recently, I opened a magazine and saw this famous woman revealing her entire body. She was about seven months pregnant and merely trying to cover her chest. I was appalled. I looked up to this woman because we are very close in age. However, I have never walked around my kids or other people for that matter without covering up.

But you know what? Society has taught these women that for them to gain money and prosperity, they have to bare it all. Why? And, for what reason? Just to sell a magazine. You're better than that. Is your self-esteem so low that you feel the need to expose yourself to the world to get attention? I think not! So, women, the next time you feel like exposing yourself to the world, talk with God first. He will tell you that your body is *His* temple, and it should be respected as such.

CHAPTER NINE

Just Messed Up

Time to put up or shut up! ***Time*** to tell the truth and shame the devil! ***Time*** to sit back, relax, and enjoy life to the fullest! Okay, so you get the point. So, what is this ***Time*** stuff all about anyway? Do you think of a ***time*** when you know you're doing wrong but continue to do it anyway?

How many ***times*** have you been in a situation where you feel eventually it must end, or you're gonna get caught? In one of my novels, *The Essence of Innocence,* the main character, Shanice Williams finds out the hard way about cheating and being caught. Let's take a look.

Here's a young lady scorned by an ex-husband contracting the aids virus and sleeping with her best friend. Her retaliation can get her into a situation where it's almost difficult to recover.

Shanice was at her ranch in Baltimore, Maryland enjoying a hot cup of cinnamon tea and watching *Lifetime Movie Network*, when her girls' ringtone lit up her cell.

"What's up girlfriend?"

Now, when Chantal Jenkins calls, Shanice listens.

"I need to talk to you. It's important. Can you come over?"

Being comfortably sitting in her chair, she jumped up. "In two minutes."

Though she knew it would take longer than two minutes, she shuddered knowing how Frank, her husband would feel about her going to Chantal's in the middle of the night. Ten minutes later, she'd put on some lipstick, combed her hair, and was halfway down I-695 heading towards Randallstown, Maryland.

She pulled up to Chantal's house and walked swiftly down the long marble driveway. Chantal was a self-made millionaire after winning the *Mega Millions* in the Maryland lottery three years prior. Being a self-made millionaire afforded her the opportunity to buy anything she wanted or needed.

Shanice knocked softly on the door. Then, she rang the doorbell.

Chantal answered smiling ear to ear. "Come in. It's so good to see you again."

Shanice took off her sweater and sat on the couch. "What's the urgency?"

"Dominique," Chantal replied frantically. "He knows about your affair with Ron. He was standing in the hallway when we were on the phone last night. He said he can't believe you would do something like that to Frank."

Shanice paused. She had met Ron on a plane a few months back while traveling from Maryland to her hometown for her cousin's funeral. Taken aback, she replied, "And us? Does he know about us?"

"Sssh," Chantal said nervously. "Not so loud. He's in the other room."

Appalled. Shanice asked, "So why did you have me come over here?"

Chantal grimaced. Then, released her smile. "We're moving to North Carolina next week."

"What? Why?" Sorrowful that she'd asked.

"Dominique got a new job and…"

"But he doesn't have to work. You guys got money flowing like honey."

"I got money, Shanice. Dominique was broke when I met him, and he will most likely be broke again if something happens to us. I made him sign a prenup."

"What? I thought only white people did that?"

"Apparently, not. Anyway, Dominique threatened to go to Frank about you and Ron."

Shanice stood up. "He's blackmailing you?"

"Kind of. I need a fresh start also. I can't be in love with a man and a woman. And look at you, you're in love with Frank, Ron, and me. We're a hot mess girlfriend!"

~

Ever been in a situation like this? Maybe it wasn't quite like this, but I'm sure you get the point. Now, what do you do about it? You're running out of time. Your world is caving in on you. You may not feel that you're doing anything wrong. However, deep inside, it bothers you knowing you have more than one person you're in love with.

So, what do you do? Well, here are some suggestions. If you're married, first you need to:

- Cut out the extracurricular activity.
- Come clean!
- Break it easy to the other person.
- Find a church and attend regularly.

If he's married and you're cheating on him and your spouse:

- **Cut him loose**—it will benefit him in the end.
- **Seek a counselor**—find someone other than a friend to cast your burdens on.

- **Tell your spouse you love them**—but that's something you'll have to decide.

- **Take some time for yourself**—rediscover who you are and what you need to do.

Many times, we get caught up in situations where it's hard to get out because one lie turns into another and it becomes habitual. Some people have told so many lies that they don't know which lie they've told to what person. If you find yourself lying regularly, ask God to help you to speak the truth. If you find yourself still lying, you must come clean. If not, it will wear you down so fast that you will eventually get caught.

So, let's see what happens next:

"Yeah, I know it's all messed up, but what's even worst, I haven't told you about Jonathan."

"Who?" Chantal's mouth flung open. "Who is Jonathan?"

Shanice twisting and turning said, "I met him about a month ago, and I just don't know what to do. I feel so skank."

"You ought to feel like *real* skank right about now. Girl, how many guys does it take to satisfy you?"

"Chantal. I just love men! Tall, dark, pale, *it don't matter.* I don't know why, but girl…"

"Shut up and listen to yourself! You're going to get caught, beat up, or killed. You gotta stop it, Shanice. You can't keep this up! How do you live with yourself?"

"It's easy for you to say. You have it all—a good man, a big house, and money for the rest of your life."

"Oh, so that's it! You're jealous of what I have?"

"No—no, that's not it at all. I can't commit to one guy. My first husband Rick hurt me so much when he and Monique messed around."

"Get over it and move on! Frank is a wonderful man. He doesn't deserve this."

"He was Monique's husband, and you know what they say, once a cheater always a cheater."

"Who cares what they say? You're better than that Shanice."

Another man in the equation? Her husband, Shanice, Ron, and now Jonathan. It's not just a messed-up situation it's disgusting. Our fictional character Shanice probably never gave thought to the:

- **Diseases she could contract**—Gonorrhea, Herpes, VD, Aids.

- **People she is hurting**—Husband, children, family and friends.

- **Her partner's partner**—Monique or any woman out there.

- **Jesus**—Her reason for living and breathing in the first place.

One thing for sure, Shanice is in a predicament and is having a heck of a time getting out of it. Amazing how the word *"time"* keeps showing up. *Time* waits for no one. You can be here today and gone tomorrow. Take *time* to love the one you're with and leave everyone else's alone. It makes for a healthy relationship, and cuts back on the mess you can get yourself into. Time also limits the lies you'd have to tell in the process.

The Saga Never Stops…

"So, you're trying to say you've never cheated before? Cause if you fix your mouth to say that, then you're a liar and a half, and your stuff sho 'nuff stinks."

Chantal burst into laughter. "Calm down girlfriend! Of course I have, but I knew when to let go."

"Fine then—since I've told you my history, I'd better tell you everything."

Chantal paused. "Do I really want to hear this?"

"It's just a lot of messed up stuff. Ron put me out because he thought I was messing with his son, and then he put me on an airplane after he had his way with me."

"Wait…wait…wait just a minute here! How could he put you out, then put you on a plane? I'm confused."

"It's a long story, but here's the gist of it. You remember when Ron came over here and found me, you, and Dominique together?"

"Yeah."

"Well, afterward he took me to his place. We made up, so I thought. He'd somehow made airline reservations in that short period—one for me, and an earlier flight for himself. When I showed up at my house, I thought Frank had moved on with another woman that fast. Then I walked in the door and saw Ron standing there. Apparently, he had told Frank that I had cheated them both."

Chantal chuckled and shook her head. "This is too much mess and drama for me. You want a beer, Wine Cooler, or Vodka? Looks like you need something girlfriend."

"It's not funny Chantal. My world is falling apart."

Shanice admits that her world is falling apart. What steps should she take to correct it?

- ***First and far most***—she should ***let go*** of everyone except her husband and find a way to reconcile with him.

- ***Seek counseling***—sometimes the only way to resolve broken trust is to seek outside help.

- ***Get tested for aids or other diseases***—if you've slept with anyone outside your spouse, you should have a yearly test for HIV or other diseases that may not go away without intensive treatment.

- ***Ask God for forgiveness in prayer***—this shows that you're sorry for your wrongdoing and may be the only hope you have.

Shanice is one of many women represented in a world of cheaters. It starts with someone cheating on you, then you get mad and cheat on them, but somehow you can't stop. You get greedy and got to have it all.

Before you run out and have secret rendezvous with different men and/or women, you need to survey the damage it would cause and the mess you'll have left behind to clean up.

Put an end to this saga…

"I'm sure it is but remember this…you got into it, now ask God to help get you out of it.

"That sounds like a plan. I'm gonna miss you—you know.

"And I'm gonna miss you too. But we'll always be girlfriends, right?"

"Always."

CHAPTER TEN

I Love Me Better Than That

Ladies, if you have not heard this song, go out and purchase it. It is a song that I've adopted for myself. Lately, I've found myself lying in bed reflecting on my life. What a life I've had! At times, I would have never thought of myself the way that I'm thinking of me right now, but the truth is, I'm no better than the girl next door. I've done some things that I'm not proud of.

In the past twenty-nine years, I have been with five different men that I always thought of it as only a hand full. While lying here recapping my life, tears are falling from the corners of my eyes. In those years, I was married twice, and that could only mean that I was unfaithful to one of my husbands. *'Anger got the best of me'* is the excuse I used. I had two men that didn't know how to love me, so I went out seeking love in all the wrong places.

The man I cheated with was a man of God that should have known better. Whoops, there I go, judging him, when I should have known better as well! I put my life in jeopardy and my marriage. Everyone talks about males being defiant and unfaithful, but come on ladies, we are just as devious if not more. It's not because we want to do this or try and trick these men. My *excuse* for cheating was loneliness and feeling unloved.

When you've been in a situation such as rape or molestation, a part of you feels like you are missing something. The sad part is that it can damage your life and the life of your family. Just ask any famous person that has been caught up in extramarital affairs. If they'd known how it would have affected their families, they probably would have stayed at home with their spouse. But possibly, they weren't getting what they wanted and considered their status to be more important than their marriage.

Often, we look to others for love and comfort when we can't find what we need at home. Maybe it's that special little something someone has told you that you haven't heard before, or maybe it's just that you don't like being with just one person. Somehow, we must look deep inside of us and say, *"I love me better than that. I can do what it takes to make my marriage or relationship work with whom I'm with."* After all, you chose that person, or they chose you for a reason. When you learn to work with what you have, you can develop a relationship with yourself. Besides, if you don't love yourself, how can you love someone else better?

Knowing how to love yourself has many qualities. Here are just a few that can help you accept yourself and return the love that you've gained to someone else:

- **Treating yourself**—Take yourself on a special trip to the spa, a mini-vacation, a bowl of ice cream, or that beautiful dress you've been wanting.

- **Stand up for what you want**—If you wait for your mate to provide for you, you're only setting yourself up for disappointment. Work hard but smartly. If you did certain things for yourself before, don't rely on a mate to bail you out. You put yourself in that mess. Don't wait for him to get you out of it. Go out and get what you want. Be proud of the woman you are.

- **Be independent**—Ladies, remember this: You don't need a man to take care of you. You're your own person. Be responsible for what it is you want in life. If a man decides he wants to take care of you, so be it. But if he figures all you want from him is to be taken care of, *he will run fast*. If you took care of yourself before the man came along, then you can take care of yourself when he gets there. Don't be afraid to treat him at times either. A man loves an independent woman that's not afraid to spend a little on him. Be persistent in what you want and do it without resolve.

CHAPTER ELEVEN

Been There Done That

Such a catchy phrase! Yet, many women have the same similarities as the woman next door. I remember growing up watching this lady being abused by a man in the community labeled, *'the root of all evil.'* Nevertheless, this man always seems to come out on top because the woman like so many women, was afraid to report the abuse or press charges. Fear, is a strong word here because women live daily with one eye closed and one foot halfway out the door, just in case their abuser comes home drunk and wants to beat their brains out.

When I was a little girl, I remember this woman being seven months pregnant and being drug from her sister's house right into the front yard. Her attacker was her boyfriend and the father of her children. He was heavily intoxicated at the time. I remember seeing him punching her and sitting on top of her. Many people tried to help her, but he was so strong. Men and women alike feared him. He shot some and stabbed others. He even chopped a woman with an ax. To date, he is still walking the streets because police officers back then were afraid of him.

On the night in question, one highway patrolman by the name of *Big John* did not fear him. When he told him to get in the car after beating the woman, he refused. That's when *Big John* smashed his head under the doorway and threw him into the car.

The woman still allowed him to come around after he got out of jail because she was afraid for her life. I often think about those days because you see that woman is no longer around, and it reminds me of some of the abuse my mother often went through with men. In society, he would be classified as a *coward* because only cowards are weak enough to beat on a pregnant and helpless woman.

Statistics show that one-third to one-half of women being abused by their spouse or boyfriend live in fear and humiliation daily. They feel intimidated and bound by their abuser. But why do women allow these men to abuse them? Most controllers come from homes where they saw their mothers being abused. They think it is okay because their fathers or the man their mothers were with, did it to control her. However, there are some cases where spousal abuse never existed in the home. Yet, sons and daughters are abusing their spouses all the time.

We live in fear daily. But the fear we live in could cause a world of pain tomorrow. Remember the phrase, *"where there's a will, there's a way."* Run for your life while you have the chance, it could be to a friend's house, your mom's house, or a safe house. But get away! Some men prey on the weakness of a woman's conscious, but God gives us strength to pray on the throne of Glory. When you need someone to turn to, you can always count on God to be your help in a time of need.

Here is a short scenario I would like you to pay attention to. Then ask yourself, "Does this sound familiar?"

Beat to Shame

He didn't mean to do it. It was my entire fault. He said he loved me. But, why? How did he get to this point? I only was five minutes late…this time. I tried to hurry back. But the traffic—it was so heavy. I knew he was waiting on his six-pack of beer. I should've hurried.

My eye… It hurt so bad. God, look at my arms! My face…so much blood. He didn't mean to do it. I know Jerry loves me. He even went out and bought me a heart necklace. Now tell me, a man spending his hard earned money on a heart necklace, doesn't love me?

I really need some help. My body hurt worse this time. My hands—they…they have these big bruises. I can't let anybody see me like this. What will my *excuse* be this time?

- I fell down the stairs. But we don't have any stairs.
- I tripped on the steps.

• Somebody jumped me on the way home.

Jerry would kill me if I left the house. He said it don't look bad. He said if I look in the mirror, he will know. I can't let him keep doing this to me. What if he kills me the next time? Got to learn how to punch back! He got to go to sleep, right? Some say hot water, grits, or even coffee…would do the trick. What can I do to make him leave me alone? He's coming back. He looks so angry. God help me!

"*Stop it, Jerry!*" No, please. I'm sorry," I screamed. "Please, don't hit me again."

"Can't you see how much I love you woman? Why you keep pushing me like this?"

He's pulling my hair—dragging me through the house like a dog on a leash.

"Please stop it, *Jerry!*"

I see something to protect me from the next punch. "Just one swing. I hope I don't hurt him that bad. He fell to the floor. He no longer has my hair. I'm free.

"Jerry—Jerry, you can get up now."

He's not responding. What to do? What to do? It was just a whack across the head. Serves him right, though. I can see my reflection now. The mirror on the wall…my face. I can't stop kicking him.

"Hello…911. You can come and get this piece of crap now. He can't hurt me anymore."

~

Ever feel like you've been pushed to the point of no return? How many times have you said you were leaving but stayed because there was nowhere else to go?

Many women and some men find themselves trapped in a situation where they feel helpless and betrayed. There is help through national hotlines and halfway houses for women facing abuse.

I've seen it so many times as a kid and as a grown woman. I too was in a situation where I felt like my world was crumbling down all around me. The good thing was it only happened once. I refused to let him get the best of me, a second time. Yeah, I remember saying, "he didn't mean to do it." I mean… What did I expect him to do? I had just told him that I slept with another man. Although it was a lie, I got tired of him accusing me of being with other men. I thought by telling him what he wanted to hear, he'd leave me alone. I was left dejected and degraded with very low self-esteem.

How many times do we as women believe there is no better life outside of the one that we're living? When we realize our potential in life, we will be able to get rid of the trash and find the jewels. There are so many fish in the sea. Yes, there are good as well as bad.

Remember this, if you go to a club looking for love you bring the club home with you. But, if you go to church, a store, or the mall, and a little old man follows you around, you know that somewhere out there, there's hope for you and the life you breathe.

You don't always have to decorate yourself in the way you dress. A man will fall in love with you regardless of your clothes. They will respect you even more if you are not exposed. However, if you dress provocatively revealing what should be treasured, he will always disrespect you and treat you as though you're the lowest person on Earth.

A clothed woman says something: Dignity, Class, Integrity, Respect, and the list goes on. I used to think I was a plain Jane until I was being sought out by little old men (well, maybe not that old) 50, 60. They helped me find myself again—my confidence level.

Wearing a lack of clothing much like entertainers such as thongs, walking the streets half-naked talking about a window seat, singing the single ladies' song, will never get respect from a man. Yes, they will find you attractive, but in their eyes, you're just a piece of activity they were hoping to find. For the lack of a better term, an easy lay.

Knowing the consequences you would suffer after being beaten up the first time, should help you realize that it will happen again and again. If you are a victim of spousal abuse, seek help immediately and find your breaking point. Leave the situation behind. Don't let anyone tell you there's no place to go or no one to turn to. Several hotlines are waiting for your phone call. You just have to make the decision to call. One of the numbers for battered women/domestic violence survivors is 1-800-334-2836.

Chapter Twelve

Hold On, Your Change is Coming

Hold on to your dreams! Your change is going to come. You can make it if you try. Don't worry about a thing! But, can we continue to hold on to broken promises or a relationship that doesn't seem to work? Maybe it's that job or old memories such as photographs, clothes, toys, magazines, or newspaper articles. Will you allow yourself to get rid of those things that are no longer relevant in your life?

"Hold on," you keep hearing. Your change is going to come. But when? How long do you have to wait for that new job, new relationship, money…, etc.? You're contemplating asking someone for the money. But you don't have a job or a way to pay them back.

Scenario #1

You have been praying, "Dear God, please bless me to pay my bills! But it doesn't seem like He hears you because your pockets are still empty, and your lights are getting ready to get turned off. Then out of the blue, you go to your mailbox, and you see a sealed envelope that you think is junk mail. But hold on! Maybe this is what you've been waiting for. You carefully open the envelope only to find a notice that if you don't pay your car note, it will be repossessed. You scream to the top of your lungs! *Why? Why? Why can't I live like others?*

You take the stack of mail into your house, and it sits on the table for days. Afraid to open the contents of the other mail, you continue to let it rest on a table. Your phone rings daily from bill collectors wanting their money. You place your head in the palm of your hands and look over at the stack of mail sitting on a table. You reach for it, praying no more notices from bill collectors. In between a magazine and a notification from a prize award, there is a certified letter from a lawyer, *'Dang,* you think, *Am I being sued?'* You open the contents to find a check for $10,000 from a relative that died years ago, naming you as a beneficiary. All you can say is, "Is this for real?"

You pick up the phone and call the lawyer's office who verifies the check is real. You start jumping, screaming, and shouting praising God. You can't stop praising Him.

~

Sometimes in life, not too often, God will allow you to go through some things to show you that He is still in control. When you allow God to take control of your life, He will show you things you've never seen before.

Scenario #2

Over the years, you've gained thirty-five unwanted pounds. No matter how hard you try, you can't get rid of the excess weight. You've been dieting and exercising for two months but only lost five pounds. Your weight started at two hundred ten pounds, and you're only 5'3" tall. You live your life in front of a TV snacking all day. At 6:00 p.m. you get dressed and go to work until 2:30 a.m.

You along with several of your girls have been working the night shift for over five years and have gained extra pounds. You didn't have time to exercise and you ate quite a bit to make the time go faster. With odds stacked against you, you're determined to get the weight off.

You haven't had a date in almost a year because you're afraid of being called, "fat." It's now Sunday morning, and you're trying to decide whether to go to church. You only have two dresses that you can squeeze comfortably into without being smothered to death. You see a black skirt and a lime green and black blouse that you can wear, that might shape your body decently.

You arrive just as prayer is being said, and an usher greets you with a smile and gives you a program. The choir sings songs that melt your heart, and you stand up to worship. You keep tugging at your tight fitted rising skirt but don't let it stop you from praising the Lord.

After church, you greet many parishioners and then a tall man comes up to you and introduces himself. You've seen him around but never asked his name.

You say, "Hi, I'm Portie."

"Hi, I'm Sam." He smiles, and you walk away.

After service, you approach the entrance to the church, he's standing there waiting for you. He leans over and whispers in your ear. "Sweetie, are you married?"

Before you can answer, you grimace and say, "I really don't think anyone would be interested in marrying, let alone, dating a big girl like me."

He smiles and says, "Big girls need loving too. Would you like to have dinner with me tomorrow night?"

Your heart flutters as you say 'yes, I would be delighted' before you can think. You've dieted, exercised, and prayed for your change to come. Now, God has blessed you with a man that doesn't care about your excess weight and is excited about taking you out to eat. Not to mention, he has a fat bank account as well.

Sometimes, when you wait patiently for a change to come, God will send a blessing your way you've never expected. What we may think is excess, someone else might think to be delightful.

CHAPTER THIRTEEN

Victim of Circumstance

How many times have you been victimized by people you thought were your friends? This includes relatives, coworkers, and strangers you've met along the way. I can recall countless days and nights that I have fallen short, to being a victim. Until I could *Let Go and Let God* take over my life, I couldn't seem to do anything but allow the enemy to tear me apart. A good friend of mine (and I, use the word *friend* loosely) told me on May 21, 2010, that I needed to *encourage myself* and stop letting people victimize me.

This all happened when some girls, not women, who used to be friends turned against me and sided with the enemy. By saying *enemy*, I'm saying, she too used to be someone I thought I knew for fifteen plus years. I figured I was doing the right thing by warning one of the girls about a new coworker that had entered our fold or shift.

The conversation was twisted, and I found myself dealing with five envious women. One—very snobby, two insecure, and another confused, but the mother of them all thought she ruled the world. She thought no one could compare to what she's accomplished being in the military or college.

Some women can be the most devious creatures that God has created. It's amazing how as I walked two laps around our compound, I had so much boggling in my mind that needed to be on paper, but now that I'm writing, the words just won't come out right.

On May 20, 2010, I went to visit our office and ran into our boss. A part of me wanted and needed to talk to him, but the other part said, "Go away and let a dead horse die." I chose to talk and wish to God I'd listened to that inner voice. After engaging in an in-depth conversation, I found out two things that shattered my world: My Boss considers me to be "Drama, *(his exact words)* and he is not willing to advance me any higher than where I am."

Knowing this, I cried from the time I left his office until my friend Cynthia spoke to me about being a victim. She told me that until I stop allowing others to victimize me, I will never experience the victory God has in store for me. She was so right. I often tell my youngest son to stop allowing the kids to pick on him at school—to stand up for himself. How can I tell him not to be a victim when that's what I am doing?

I had every intention of going to work and having a final talk with these ladies, but God intervened and brought

Cynthia on (who by the way, was not scheduled to work with us—but was filling in for someone on leave) to lift my spirits and help me. Now, I can let whatever the devil tried to steal from me through evil intentions, dissipate as if it never existed.

It's amazing how God intervenes in our lives. Just when we think He doesn't care, He makes His presence known and helps us take back what the devil stole from us—our pride and integrity.

Are you a victim of circumstance? Have you allowed yourself to be victimized by family, friends, or people you don't really know that well? Then, you need to take a stand. Don't rehash the past! *Don't revisit old flames!* Let them go! If you go back to where you began, you will always allow yourself to be a victim of circumstance.

Remember, the devil is the author of confusion,
if we allow him to take control,
then we are no different than the one who brought you down in the first
place.

Defeated

July 2010

Ever reached the end of your rope? Feel like nothing is going your way? God, "Why? What? And how did it come to this?" We've all done it. No matter how many times you are told not to question God, you do it anyway. It's by habit. We are human. We all do it.

Many things can cause you to reach the end of your rope. For instance:

- **A Nasty Divorce**—You always fight over kids that both of you created together. I don't understand the problem. The kids belong to the both of you, so why are you fighting over who gets what weekends? You tend to hold a grudge because he or she left you for someone else. Get over it! So, they didn't want you. It's their loss, not yours. You should never deny your ex the right to see their child or children whenever they want to. When I got my divorce, I made sure that my ex-husband was given privileges to see his boys whenever he wanted to. I wasn't going to let anyone especially the government tell me when he could see them. That's bull crap! These are his boys also. Stop the hatred ladies and move on! Remember this, if your child knows that you are the cause of them not seeing their daddy or mommy, they will resent you later.

- **Loss of job**—You finally settled into your new house, bought a new car, and planned the family you've always dreamed of. Your Boss walks in and tells you the budget is being cut and you're the last hired. Your spouse doesn't work. Unemployment will not pay the bills. You've reached the end of the funds in your bank account and have run up all your credit cards. You have no one to turn to.

- **The person you love doesn't love you back**—No matter what you do, you can't seem to please your significant other. You go out of your way to do things you think are important and they don't acknowledge you. You try and hang in there in hopes that it would get better, but you're being placed on the shelf like all the other trophies they've won.

- **You've had a bad day**—Your hand's been hurting for over three weeks. You go to the triage at the Veteran's Administration. They give you some cream for arthritis, back pain, and muscle aches. You're diagnosed with damaged nerves in your hand. As soon as you put the capsaicin cream on, you start to cough. Your reflexes tell you to cover, therefore, causing you to put your hands over your mouth and your whole freakin' mouth and face are on fire. You're screaming up a storm. You have about ten minutes before you get home. You reach your house, throw your car in park, and run to the bathroom. You grab a rag, soap, and lots of water and finally get it under control. Whew! You're thanking God, and asking Him why you must endure so much pain and suffering if you're His child?

- **Facial Madness**—It's 6:47 p.m. and you just fixed the kids something to eat, and go to work at 10:00 p.m. You jump back up thinking you should put more cream on your hands while you're asleep. You separate your hands from your face and start dreaming. It was a good one too. However, we know all good things tend to come to an end. You start to choke while sleeping and immediately place hand—cream and all—in your face and your eyes. Now, you're screaming again because the cream has your eyes on fire. You're running through the house calling your oldest son to assist you. He grabs a big cup of water and wants to pour it into your eyes. After nearly twenty minutes, you call the Veteran's ER, and suddenly you finally ease the pain. You think to yourself, "What is going on?" You just knew your face would be damaged forever. You're so grateful God spared you.

Sometimes, when we've endured so much, God will step in and tell the devil, "That's enough!" I felt my defeat—my end of the rope. But, I'm so glad God prevailed and spared my life once again. Unfortunately, my hand hasn't stopped hurting, and my face still is tingling in different spots. You can bet, I won't use that cream again.

I felt my defeat that night, but then I spoke with an older gentleman the next morning named Harry. He came in at 3:00 a.m. for a moment. It wasn't his regular time, but God sent him there to tell me something. He complimented my hands, and I laughed. I told him how my hands had been hurting for over three and a half weeks. He said that I had beautiful hands and immediately, I went into defense.

"Ewe," I have the ugliest hands in the world."

He then responded with, "*sometimes, it's the beauty in your heart that makes your hands look beautiful.*" I started to tear up just trying to accept his compliment.

Then, he commenced to saying, "I want you to do something for Donna today. No one else but Donna. Turn the phone, TV, and Radio off and listen to your heart. Treat yourself to something special."

Now, I'm floored. What an Angel! When my good friend came to look at my hand, Harry was standing there. My friend had to walk away because duty called. But Harry stayed and made me feel like I was special not defeated after all.

Angels are all around us. I call my mother my biggest angel although she has been dead for over eight years. Her spirit has been here all along. Mama inspired me while she was alive. Anytime I felt defeated or at the end of my rope, I could always call on her, and she always knew the right words to say. Though I miss her dearly, I could not have made it this far without her love and support.

There's a saying about people being in your life for a reason, season, and lifetime. Mama, was all those things for me. Take the time and find your special Angel. When you feel like you can't go on, and at the end of your rope or defeated—Remember this: God placed a special Angel in your life just for you.

CHAPTER FOURTEEN

Holding a Grudge

Ever held a grudge for so long that you cannot remember why you were holding on to it in the first place? Has it been a year, five, ten or more? Then you need to get over it. Life is too short. I held a grudge for so long against my former brother-in-law that it took him lying in a casket for me to open my eyes.

In fact, I had the audacity to look down at him and say, "I forgive you." To a dead man—he was dead already! I felt like crawling under a rock and beating myself upside the head with it. He told a lie that disrupted my family that ended in a divorce. Wow! Don't let that happen to you. He was indeed a good guy, but I felt like he stirred up some mess a few times in my marriage, and it caused me and my ex-husband to drift apart.

My ex-husband tended to believe what everyone said but his own wife. I guess that's why I held a grudge with my him for over ten years. He always seemed to say that I held on to the past, but when the pain is never resolved, it's almost impossible to get over it. I always tell people '*I hold hurt not grudges,*' but we all know pain doesn't last a lifetime, but not forgiving does.

So, there you are—you, your husband, and your then five-year-old son at your sister-in-law's, after a year and a half in Panama. You're having fun and the time has wound down. It's after 3:00 a.m. in the morning and your other sister-in-law decides to crash where you are supposed to be sleeping. You wait until she settles down and you blow up the full-size air mattress you purchased for your mother. You will be leaving for Pensacola, Florida in a couple days and you're excited. After blowing up your mattress, the next thing you see is your sister-in-law prancing back and forth on top of it like she doesn't have the sense God gave her. So, you're standing with your mouth gaped and eyes in a daze, in awe wondering '*what is her problem?*'

So, you say, "If you'd asked me to move the mattress, I would have gladly moved it!"

She fixed her face and replied, "I had one of these and people broke mine."

I responded with, "But I was not that person, and this belongs to my mother."

Before I could finish, my then-husband said, "Sis you can walk on that mattress anytime you want to, you're pregnant."

I was floored. It's been almost thirteen years, and I have still been carrying that grudge. I used to say that I was hurt, knowing deep inside I was hotter than fish grease!

Now that I'm finally free from him and his undying love for his family, I raise my hands to the sky and say, *'Hallelujah, Thank You, Jesus!'* I don't know why it took me so long to walk away from him. Maybe it was the love I have for my kids that kept me there. Or perhaps, I felt sorry for him. Don't get me wrong. I will always care for my ex-husband because he gave me—two of the most beautiful intelligent boys in the world.

When we hold grudges against the ones we love, we miss out on a lot of quality time with our family. I literally stopped going to see them as often as I had, and he always made excuses as to why I didn't go. We as people must learn to let go of the things we cannot control and let God take better control of our lives.

Remember this: Holding grudges not only hurts the ones you love or the person you're holding a grudge against, but it also hurts you. Before life passes you by, make amends with those you love or care about. You never know when it might be the last time you see them, or they see you.

CHAPTER FIFTEEN

In Love with the Wrong Man

PORTUGUESE

Ladies, how many times have you sold yourself short knowing you were in love with one man, but settled for someone else? What about dating or marrying someone you thought was God's gift to women? Then, he got complacent and stop taking you out to eat, buying you unique gifts, or kissing you in all the right places?

Imagine heading home from work and you stopped by the store to pick up few things. You pull up in the parking lot and your key to destiny is waiting for you. You stepped outside your RX7 that's parked next to a black Lexus convertible and Mister Right now is standing as close as your fingertips. You suckle in a deep soothing breath as you feel a breeze brush the side of your hair. He gives you a slight wink, and you trip over yourself trying to make it in the store before he says a word.

Two minutes later, your shopping carts meet head on. You're no longer secured in freedom but entangled by the glowing hazels sparkling in the center of his forehead. You can't see past his eyes luring you away from your shopping. You try to walk away from him without a glimmer of a smile, but he grabs hold of your arm and says, "Kenneth, and you are?"

Before you can think, you reply, "Journey, waiting for you to take me on one." Then you realize for the life of you that you've let this man know you're available and not afraid to speak your mind.

His smile gazes past the speck of frosting left on your cheek. He reaches toward you, but you flinch not knowing what he has on his mind.

"I hope the cake was good," he says with a smile.

Then you realize why he reached towards your face. You'd just eaten a piece of cake before leaving home and must have gotten some icing on your face. You think, *'Great! I meet the finest man on Earth wearing pink and white frosting on the left side of my cheek.'*

Embarrassed that you've finally met mister look so good and he spots frosting on your cheek, you make a quick dash towards the front of the store, but he beats you to the exit.

"I didn't mean to frighten you. I just want to know how I can get with a woman like you?"

Shivering—you respond, "I just got out of a bad situation. I'm not trying to start another."

Defeated, he throws his hands up. But we all know, no man takes 'no' for an answer the first time. So, clever, and smooth Kenneth says, "If you must go, I guess I'll have to respect that, but all I want is a little of your time."

Then you feel guilty not giving the brother the time of day, so you cave. "Well, I guess it's okay," you say twirling a finger around the nape of your hair.

You exchange numbers. He gives you a card that says, 'Kenneth Eldridge, President, and CEO of Eldridge & Associates.'

You think to yourself, *'I've scored a lawyer.'* Then you pat yourself on the back, all the while smooth talking Kenny has reeled in his fifth woman in two days.

You go home, call every girlfriend you know and tell them how you've just met the man of your dreams. Two weeks later, you're sitting at the River House Restaurant in North Augusta, South Carolina ordering an eight-ounce Filet Mignon with Roasted Potatoes and Veggies topped with Mushroom Sauce. Then, he pulls out an 18 Carat Diamond Bracelet, and you almost fall out of your seat with excitement, not even checking to see if Kenneth is going to give it to you. But in your mind, it's already yours.

You extend your wrist pulling up your shirt sleeve towards the back of your elbow. He fastens the bracelet around your wrist and watches the shimmering smile race across your face. Before you know it, you're saying, 'I love you, Kenneth,' and you've allowed him to come over for a nightcap.

After several months of wining and dining, you're beside yourself when Kenneth brings out the engagement ring and wants to get married. You can't see past the dollar signs, and once again you're trapped in another relationship leading to a path of destruction.

It's been a year and the man you married no longer resembles the man you fell in love with. He's no longer President and CEO of Eldridge & Associates. He's swindled all the funds from his account trying to keep you happy and has lost his job in the process. He's no longer smooth Kenneth, but a couch potato with a loaded sack of blubber playing video games all day. The house is filthy, the clothes need washing, dishes are stacked, and you're expecting a child in three months. Your salary won't cover the bills because you are only an office assistant. The mortgage is due, the bills haven't been paid, and Kenny is snorting cocaine with his friends.

Reality has slapped you in the face, and you are at the end of your rope about to fall off. The man you thought you fell in love with pretended to be someone he was not. *Oops! You've done it again—fell in love with the wrong man.*

How many times have we fallen into what we thought was love, but was only lust? A man might have riches one day and dirt poor the next. If we search for a heart of gold, we'll find treasure at the end of the rainbow. If we search for money, power, and prestige, we'll find hurt, pain, and empty pockets. Take the time to *fall for the heart* and not the monetary benefits it can provide. Having diamonds and pearls doesn't mean you'll have happiness forever.

Problems:

- Opposites attract attention.
- Don't let the glimmer ruin the relationship.
- Sour grapes produce rotten raisins.

Solution:

- Know what you are seeking before you find it.

A Broken Relationship

Have you ever wondered why your kids don't respect you the way they used to? A guy just stopped and talked to me about his ex-wife. I wasn't too shocked at what he said but at an alarming rate, women more so than men gain custody of children if the relationship or marriage has gone sour.

I believe I addressed this earlier, but there is a need to reiterate it again. We as parents must stop trying to manipulate our children into hating the other parent. It's not their fault that the two of you couldn't cut it, so don't make them feel like it was.

Another issue that bothers me more than anything is the *'father will see them every other weekend'* or *'the mother won't let him see them at all.'* When, did these children become the prize? You created them together. They didn't ask to be here. Therefore, it shouldn't be any fuss over who gets them or when. They should never be denied either parent.

So, here's what you should do:

- Involve Christ in your daily routine.

- Sit down like responsible adults and talk about things that concern the family.

- Explain to your children that mommy and daddy love them more than anything but can't work things out.

- Remain friends regardless of if someone else has entered the equation. If they cannot fathom the thought of you being friends, explain to them the concept of being a family and how important it is for you to remain friends for your child's sake.

- Seek counseling or better yet, write down the good and bad things you like or dislike about each other.

- Leave other people out of your relationship.

If you decide to leave, make sure things are in order such as the house, etc. If the bills are in your name, switch them to your new address, or have your name taken off before leaving.

One of my biggest mistakes was trusting and believing that my ex-husband was going to refinance the house and give me a portion of what he got. I didn't put it in the divorce decree to divide the profit equally. Unfortunately, when he gained possession of the house, he left me high and dry. I also felt sorry for him and told the judge he didn't have to pay me full child support and a couple months later, he got a huge raise, and I'm left struggling. Be sure you specify what you want out of the marriage so that in the end, you won't be left looking like a silly woman.

Also, a significant factor is joint custody. Since your children love the both of you, don't make them choose between you. You're grown and should be able to come to reasonable terms of allowing him or her to see their children every day. *'Yes, I said every day.'*

I work at night, so there is no one else I trust enough to leave my son with other than my ex. On the weekends, I will allow him to choose who he wants to be with, but he has to be with either parent whether it's on a Friday or Saturday. This way, the child still interacts with the both of you and will do better in school. Children are a vital part of our future. If not nurtured properly, their future could be drastically altered, if not ruined altogether.

Remember this: A friendly environment today means a better household tomorrow.

CHAPTER SIXTEEN

Never Deny Yourself

Sometimes as humans, we like to take the lazy days and just lay around without a care in the world. But these days, it's hard to find someone who is looking for a mate that wants a person who does nothing but sit around and watch TV all day. No matter how small it seems, such as going to the movies, a ball game or even to the gym, there should always be movement in your relationship. But we make the same excuses such as:

- I'm tired.

- Let's set weekly dates.

- My head, back, or stomach aches.

'No,' should never be a part of your vocabulary when it comes to being with the one you love. Eventually, your mate will get tired and start looking elsewhere. And, I know you wouldn't want that. But in essence, we should be like robots using Energizer batteries. They take a licking but keep on ticking.

One of the biggest pet peeves I have in a relationship is meeting someone and then finding out they weren't the person you were looking for. For instance, say you were window shopping and all of a sudden, this nice-looking man comes up to you and says, "If I had a woman like you, you wouldn't have to look in the window at that dress, I'd make sure you were wearing it already."

You grimace saying to yourself, *'Is he kidding me? I know what's on his mind, and it ain't happening here.'* But you humor yourself and say, "Well, I only look in the window because payday isn't until Friday and I seek out my purchases before I make them."

See, now he already figured you out. He knows that you want that dress, but you have to wait for it.

So, he says, "Listen, sweetheart, don't ever deny yourself of life treasures especially when it is staring you in the face. If you see something you want, make an attempt to possess it."

Now that was smart thinking on his part. An intelligent person whether it is a man or woman comes a dime a dozen. You must decide when you want something to happen. But was this the time to make that decision?

What if you are already involved with someone but they haven't been the caring person you thought they were when you first met? Would you let that person go for someone with smooth lines?

A good question indeed, and it's totally up to you to decide whether to start a new relationship. Given that he just said if you were with him that you would be wearing what you want, already.

So, let's look deeper into that because it seems like this could be a great fit for you. How often has the person you've been dating (not married to) tell you to go into a store and get what you like? Was it sincere or was it with an attitude? There is a big difference. A genuine smile along with an arm around the waist is an honest effort. However, if the smile was to the side of the face, you have a problem.

Now that he has your attention, what are you going to do about it? Well, here's a little advice before you make that decision. Although your significant other doesn't get the idea of you wanting that dress today, he may have a mink coat in the closet for your birthday or Christmas. Remember, material things are somewhat important and if you have someone that's slow about getting things done, leaving may not be the solution, but don't deny yourself of life's possibilities.

CHAPTER SEVENTEEN

Not Your Ordinary Stuff

By now, most of you know who I am and how my mind operates. I would be remittent if I couldn't add a taste of who I am and what my heart desires in the series of *"Finding Me, Finding You."* It started as a child and ended as an adult driven by my passion for writing, my fulfillment to make others laugh, and my dream to find the person God intended me to be. It pleases me the most when people come up to me and say, "I've read your books and how can I get a hold of the other ones?"

Let me take you on a fictitious journey as only I can do. As you know, it starts with an addiction. It doesn't have to be a drug or alcohol addiction. The kind I'm talking about is only in your dreams. It can happen any time at home, the mall, or even at work. This addiction started at work. Have you ever seen someone at work that your mind wouldn't let go of?

Addition . . . Only in Her Dreams

She watched him walk through the tan wooden door, glancing at him with eyes of innocence and hoping she would catch his attention. She imagined how it would feel just to be able to talk to him. She was a reclusive woman with a son that loved to play ball. She worked all day and needed someone to call her own at night. Yet, she sat staring at the empty door that whisked his presence from existence. Patiently, she waited for his return. Seeing his face would make the evil that she worked with go away.

She was a laughing stalk to the women she worked with. Men didn't pay attention to her because she didn't have a beautiful body or long hair like the rest of them although they paid for it. She was much older, and they were still in their early twenties. She sat there reading a book she had gotten from one of her coworkers. No one in sight but the crickets chirping, roaches flying and spiders crawling.

So, there she sat pondering over the things that were most important in her life: Family, food, God *(which should've been first)*, and her job. Yet, she allowed herself to get caught up in the fantasy of a man that existed only in her mind.

Then, he appeared wearing his blue police uniform with a sparkling badge. He was tall, dark, and very handsome. He's fully armed as he made his rounds throughout the building disappearing once again. Her heart pounded wanting to see more of him. *She sighed.*

'Patience,' she told herself.

She inhaled, then, let it out slowly. Her anxiety was getting the best of her. She pulled out her inhaler. '*Nice deep breaths,*' she had to tell herself. She had an addiction every time she saw the man of her dreams, but too scared to say something. It was like an addiction a druggie has needing a blunt, but not being able to afford it.

He tiptoed past her pretending not to see her staring through the mirrored windows. As she stood, shades of charcoal, violet, and lime peering back at her as she heard two more voices whispering through the air. The one—dressed in black with dark skin wearing a pair of Calvin Klein eyeglasses. The other—a Caucasian thinned frame with bumpy skin. But the one she adored didn't acknowledge her.

'*Ughhh*—the agony of waiting,' she silently screamed. Her hope blossomed when suddenly the tan door opened wide, and he saw her. Nearly tripping over herself, she panted. "Oh—oh—oh!" Rapidly fanning herself. 'Yes, yes, yes—it's him,' she chuckled telling herself to calm down. She turned slightly to the side so that he can see her peering at him.

He smiled.

She said, "Ummm hmmm."

He responded the same disappearing once again into the door of the unknown.

She stared at the color of her rosy nail polish plastered onto her nails. It must have meant a lot to have them done. For she always tends not to engage in the fascination of deception.

Hours have gone by, and the tall dark one has not opened the door to her heart. The metaphors of pacing the floor, astounding aphrodisiac driving her crazy with the inveigle perception of wanting something she cannot have.

A soft mellow sound illuminated through the airwaves. Cymbals vibrating as the rhythmical flow of vocals diluted the gray box behind her. Florescent lights guiding her imagination as she waited for mister tall, dark, and handsome to make his appearance.

'God help me!' She was an addict—stalker of desire! Lover of emotions! Graced by the powers of seeing someone she couldn't have.

Her contemptuous disparity poured through the windows of sorrow.

"Where is he?" She screamed with intense reformed gratification.

So, she sat—wanton and waiting, addicted by the sight of his mere presence. Her luminous eyes started to glow. It's 4:37 a.m. and she finally sees the dark stranger standing at the tan door.

"Hello there," he says making her quiver.

Finally, hours after longing for him to say something other than, "Ummm hmmm," he spoke. She jolted, melting with an addiction of circumstance she'd held buried inside. "My God! You actually spoke to me," sweating profusely.

A loud noise—what was it? A ringing tone jingling in her ears. Once again, she had awakened from a recurrence that finally got her to the point of a mere, *"Hello."*

"That stupid alarm clock!" She ranted fighting the pillows underneath her head struggling to return to her addiction.

It all vanished from her sight and her memory.

Second Night

As she tossed and turned in the empty bed of disparity, she found herself walking down a long dismal path listening to the sounds of weary creatures chirping in the tall grassy furnace beside her. The darkness of the clouds and rumbling of thunder increased as she picked up the pace with her tired feet.

A tall shadow appeared and yet, it's not the right one her heart thrived for. Just another passerby waving feverishly at her. She returned the greeting smirking to herself. If only the tall dark one knew why the huge smile encountered her face, as she entered the building adjacent her, he would come to see her more often.

"I'm here to gather my belongings," she gleefully announced as the watchman sat at her seat reading the latest edition of *Sport's Illustrated*.

Beautiful and quiet. No one other than her sitting in an empty room counting down the hours of freedom before she could be set free.

She made her way across the black asphalt padding underneath her feet. Hoping the sky would quiet itself and the rain would hold steady until she was settled.

She trotted through the gated bars and sat comfortably in the black leather chair waiting for her relief. There he was, the tall dark one, coming around the corner of desire. Happiness encountered her mind. Pounds of grief lifted from her shoulders after leaving her heart beating faster than the average computer hard drive. She was grateful that he wasn't shying away from her. He walked towards her. She tensed. Would he say something to her this time or just walk away like he normally does?

When her assistant came back, she grabbed what was needed and walked slowly with him.

'*Beep…beep…beep* — "No, no, nooo… not again." She pouted. "This can't be happening." But she refused to wake up. She wouldn't allow herself the satisfaction of losing another night's sleep over him.

Five more minutes was all she allowed herself to find the tall dark one. He was there. Still walking beside her, he didn't say a word until she finally couldn't take it anymore.

"Do you have a name?" Her heart pleading for an answer.

He snickered. "I do, but if I tell you, I'll have to…"

'*Beep, beep, beep*'—the alarm clock screamed again, "Oh My *God!* This is not happening!!!" She tried to find him once again but no matter her plight, she couldn't.

"Why?" She muttered and went about her busy day.

Night Three . . . Finding Him

The intensity deepened. She hurried herself to sleep. She had to find him. She'd just had a fight with her significant other. He's got to be around. And—yet, he was.

She jumped in her car and sped down the road of destruction as fast as she could. She was successful in getting his number, but somehow must've missed that segment in her dreams. She didn't remember that portion at all, but was ecstatic to have the digits. It was like a soap opera—a constant reoccurrence of personal events in one's life.

She high-tailed down the road doing sixty or so.

'No, I won't call him,' she proclaimed. But he said she had an open invitation to his heart. But she thought it meant to his house. *In her creative mind,* that's what it was supposed to be. The digits on the phone seem to take forever to dial. It's not as if she had him on speed dial or anything crazy like that.

"Hello," knowing he was finally on the phone with her. "You said I had an open invitation."

"I did say that, didn't I?" She could feel a part of her lighting up knowing he'd allowed her access to his kingdom.

'I won't give in if he tries to lure me,' she proclaimed. Her mind was thinking ahead of her thoughts.

He opened the door. His man cave was scary. Swords were Criss—cross on his purplish walls. Helicopters were dangling from his ceilings. Sheets instead of curtains sealed tightly against the windowpanes. *Wow!* What had she gotten herself into? But hey—it was only a dream—her fantasy, right? Wrong, the dream had turned into reality. He was real. She could reach out and touch him. She had conjured up the tall, dark one from her sleepless nights into her bright days of hope.

He didn't attack her, even though she inwardly desired his advances. He only wanted to comfort her sorrows and help release what was ailing her.

"Don't cry," his voice was like deep running waters that soothed her soul. She tried not to pour out her terrible life to him, but she was lonely and in need of a friendly ear. So, there she sat teary eyed and very needy. He sat next to her pulling out his computer. It was enough to let her know she had utterly bored him to death.

Two days later, she found herself needier and wanton of him. She called on him once again desiring a sympathetic ear. He listened intently. She went over to his man cave. He placed his arm around the back of her neck. She had to leave quick! Though she wanted to know him, she wasn't ready for a relationship with him. She still had her son to take care of. After all the chasing in her dreams, she simply, wasn't ready.

Then it happened! A tiny voice whispering in her ear. "We're gonna be late."

"God nooo," she screamed! It was a dream. Awakened by the nagging voice of *'momma—momma, we're gonna be late for my football game.'*

"It was a dreadful dream," she murmured. Growling at her very existence. Eight years, two months, one week and seven hours of loving the most precious *gift* God had given her, and yet, she hungered for more.

"I'm getting up now," she told the waiting crumb snatcher pounding the sides of her now aching face.

"Get up Mommy! Get up! I'm gonna miss the game," he declared anxiously.

"Yeah, and I'm going to miss one of the best dreams that's ever happened to me," she responded forgetting he was only eight.

"Mom," his words echoed through her ears. Then and only then did she realize that she had to break free of her midnight fantasies.

They got in her car driving top speed. She arrived with one minute to spare. He dashed putting on his gear.

Her next stare sent blossoms throughout her body. Reality. She was short of saying, "When I see you," my heart goes pitter-patter. But he knew not of her, for it was merely a dream of desire that would not come true for her.

The beautiful woman wearing a big 24-karat gold ring seated next to him was his wife of three years. She overheard her telling one of the women seated next to her as she flashed her big diamond ring. Her gaping mouth finally closed and sadly, she walked to the other side of the bleachers. A single tear dropped from her eye, and she knew she had to recover from the addiction draining her mind nightly. She pulled herself together declaring that since she'd seen the tall, dark one, he'd be finally erased from her dreams.

Sometimes we can't face reality because our minds are still stuck in a dream of desire that will never come true.

CHAPTER EIGHTEEN

Unhappily Ever After

I remember hearing, "Hey beautiful, you want to go steady," echoing through the bright yellow school bus taking us back home from school? I smiled not knowing what going steady meant at the time, but I was anxious to find out. His eyes were widespread, and his mouth gaped awaiting my response. I kept him waiting a few more minutes because everyone was staring at me. I turned towards him and said, "Yeah," then shyly turned around in my seat facing the people on the crowded bus.

My eyes illuminated the day he asked if I would be his girl. I was fourteen and knew my mother would kill me if I were to try dating a guy before I was finished with high school. He being a seventeen-year-old boy, meant that he was almost grown and could have easily gotten in trouble for statutory rape of a minor. We dated secretly until I couldn't hide it anymore from my mom. I told her about him, and she surprisingly wasn't upset. He had already signed up for the Army before we started dating and it broke my heart when he left. They sent him straight to Fort Knox, Kentucky. Then, off to Germany. Every time he returned, I would light up. He wasn't the most attractive young man, but he seemed to be kind. I was raring to leave momma's house but didn't really want to.

We had been dating for six years, and like many young girls, I made the mistake of trying to grow up too fast. I wanted freedom but as people always said, *"freedom comes with a price."* I moved from a crowded house to a smothered place. I wasn't allowed to have male friends and God forbid if one spoke to me! I had to be sleeping with him.

I'll never forget the day we were in the mall in Pensacola, Florida and as we were about to leave, a man turned around to look at me. My then husband looked at him and said, "Man yo' eyes retarded?" How embarrassing! I felt controlled and fearful at the same time.

Many times, we allow people to take control of our lives. We fear their appearance, voice, or demeanor. We've let them tell us where we can or cannot go. Who we can and cannot see; or, even when we can and cannot see our parents once we've moved from our haven of protection.

We feel trapped—confused by the position they've placed us in. Have you been told that no one will love you as he or she would? Did you wake up one morning feeling like someone stole your joy? Then, you are like I was, *Unhappily Ever After*. It will never change unless you make the first step.

Did you know that being married can cause you to be *Unhappily Ever After*? That day you say the words, "I do" can be the best and worst day of your life. Just because he gave you a huge ring and promised you a lifetime of happiness doesn't mean it will be so.

So, you're all prepared to be married on a hot summer's day, and sweat is pouring down your face so much that your makeup has smeared and your eyeliner has you looking like a clown. By the time you're ready to walk down the aisle, you look like a drag queen on a bad day.

Even so, you're ecstatic because you're marrying your childhood beau, your high school sweetheart. You were inseparable.

After the wedding, your mom comes to you and tells you that she just saw your husband with your so-called best friend and they were cozied up in the dining hall like they were a married couple. You brush it off and tell her to mind her business and stay out of yours. Later that night, you approach him about it while you are supposed to be on your honeymoon, and he attacks you with a huge slap in the face. You grab your face like you're in total shock, but all along he had been abusing you, and you never said a word.

You've never lived together until now and all the promises he made went out the window. Now you're married, trapped, and scared to breathe. Then one day out of the blue, he announced he wants to move you away from your family and friends you've grown to love your entire life. You gasped loudly feeling like someone has placed a noose around your neck, choking you so that you cannot break free.

For nearly two months, you're on pins and needles hoping for a breakthrough. You see a commercial on TV for the military and prepare to leave once he goes to work. You contact a recruiter and hope they can get you out of the situation sooner rather than later. You're in luck, and they've found a job suitable for you. Then you wait for him to go to work a week later and you pack your bags, leave a Dear John letter behind, and file for a divorce. You've only been married for two months and wonder if people would laugh at you for giving up so soon. Actually, they were just as happy as you were.

For most women, it's not this easy to get out of an abusive relationship. Sadly, most women stay and take the punishment from men because they believe they have nowhere else to go. But you see, I'm a different type of woman. I don't allow any men to abuse me. I will walk away and think nothing of it.

Some men feel there is power in trying to control a woman. That's their leverage in keeping you bound to them.

Sometimes, men can make us feel like we owe them something because they gave us a life we've never had before. But, at what cost do we have to show our gratitude?

Don't be a statistic! If he hit you once, you better believe, he'll hit you again. Get out while you still can. Don't make excuses!

Make yourself a promise, grab your possessions, and get out!

CHAPTER NINETEEN

Office of My Affection

Nightly, she watched as they walked passed her desk snickering and holding hands. He was Caucasian in the Air Force—She African-American in the Army. The glare between them was phenomenal. Where he went, she trailed behind. They were young early twenties and bored. Back and forth, they walked all night.

One night as she watched the door to the secretive room, they bore flung open sweat draining from their faces. Her hair was short in length black in color—coarse by nature. His military cut sides trimmed high. They smiled knowing they'd been caught, but never reported.

For weeks, their love intensified. The office began to have a funny smell almost like a rat had died in a corner, and no one noticed it. Co-workers sensing something lascivious had taken place, set up a camera to view the activity during the week. They could find nothing outside a co-worker removing a pen from his desk and putting it in the pocket on his shirt.

Then, by chance, a colleague suggested setting up a nightly camera as well. The first couple of nights nothing took place. Word spread throughout the office of paranoia. The boss—Caucasian—relied on his crew to come up with a solution. The smell had gotten worse. But no one could figure it out. Then a single spot lay on the floor. Clear and dry.

"Nah," one of them said. "It couldn't be." But there it was, plain as day—one little speckle. No one dares to touch or wipe it away. First, it was thought to be from an insect, but the smell was futile. A single drop of liquid rested near the corner of a mahogany desk.

The small drop had to be analyzed. For someone in the office had broken the rules. Silence became them as everyone glared hazily at each other, wondering who, would have the audacity to come to work and do such a thing in broad daylight. "But what if it wasn't during the day?" John said. Management watched closely for the tell-tale faces in the room. No one budged.

"The night shift," someone uttered. "Only Tim and Meka work the night shift. But it couldn't be. They had nothing in common. She was dark—He pale."

"Hmmm, maybe they just are obsessed with each other," Gloria Roberts, head secretary grimaced.

"One way or another, we have to get to the bottom of this. An incident like this could ruin the company," Mr. Henry, the chief executive officer of the firm replied.

Seemingly, Tim and Meka arrived thirty minutes before their shift. They were already worked up about being together. Tonight, however, would be different. They had to have a different location, a better plan. Conference Room "C" on the east wing stayed available all night.

Tim Hopkins arrived at the post calm and overwhelmingly giddy. The key to conference room "C" was tucked away in the gray box hanging on the wall. Tim politely said hello and requested the key. He told the receptionist that he had a special presentation he had to give and wanted to get set up for a meeting.

Tim took the key, and Meka met him around the corner. She pretended to duck into the women's bathroom. A code knock on the door and she was in!

Gloria made a special trip to the office that night. All was quiet, but Tim and Meka weren't in sight. "Weird," she thought to herself knowing they should have been at work. Gloria got back in the elevator stopping on the first floor. She asked the receptionist if she had seen either of them.

"Tim," she said, "came to get the key to conference room "C." She told Gloria what Tim said about a briefing he had to prepare for.

Suspicious, Gloria called Mr. Henry who made it over in record time breaking every speed limit there was to break. Together, they retrieved the master key. When they arrived, they were ready for just about anything.

Slowly, they opened the door and to their surprise, Tim, Meka, and the entire day shift were awaiting their arrival.

"Surprise," they all shouted nearly sending Mr. Henry into cardiac arrest. "Happy Birthday!"

Puzzled, he pulled Gloria aside and said, "But I thought you stated that they were in the conference room breaking the rules."

"Mr. Henry," Gloria snickered. "Do you really believe that they would actually risk their jobs to go against company policy?"

He laughed. "It is kind of ridiculous, isn't it?"

He walked over thanking everyone. Tim and Meka wiped their foreheads. The next night, they were back in their office, but this time, they were more careful. No one ever brought up the smell again.

~

Though this is a fictional tale, we all know that this kind of activity takes place daily in the workplace. Have you been caught up in the office of affection? Are you guilty of seeking out that special someone in your office?

If you can answer any of these questions with a sincere "yes," then you are amongst the group of people needing to break away from your office and get a life. Office romance never last, and once you start to engage in a relationship with a coworker, the entire office will get in your business, and the affair will spread like wildfire.

Most companies frown against workplace romances, because it can cause friction, especially if a manager or supervisor is involved, it can result in fraternization costing you your job. Think about what's important: Job security or termination for going against office policies.

If you plan on having an inappropriate relationship with someone in your office, make sure you count the cost before you spend a dime! Deception can be expensive.

All Alone

Quietly, I sat in a blurry room

Waiting for my change to come

Stillness flourished in the openness of darkness

No bright skies or shiny lights

No one but me and my lonely heart

Whispering in silence

Why me? Why now?

No signs of life . . . No hope of disparity

No one to justify the quiet tune my heart wished for

My mind racing one hundred miles per minute

Crickets chirping loudly outside my window pane

Critters crawling swiftly across the wooden floor

Yet, I'm all alone in a world

Where dreams vanish away in the night

And fantasies flourish through the minds of dreamers

Guidance from another source

Rush through the emptiness my heart desire

Yet, I stay locked up in my own world

Hoping someday my empty heart

Would flourish to a blossoming spring

All alone by myself

CHAPTER TWENTY

Talking Yourself out of a Relationship

Ever had a good thing going and blew it because you spoke too much? Whether it was about a past relationship, loneliness, depression, or even lack of confidence in yourself? If you said yes to this, then you are not alone. I once asked a good friend of mine for his honest opinion of me and what he said took me aback. He told me that I have very low self-esteem, I'm always down on myself, I take on too many problems that are not mine, and the list went on and on.

These are some of the things that could cost you a relationship that you've worked years to gain. With me being recently divorced, I find myself talking to men about my ex-spouse and other relationships that I've had. Though it may not bother me, I'm sure after a while they get tired of hearing about it and start to drift away.

One friend told me that he didn't meet up with me to talk about another man. He could have stayed home if he'd known I would be talking about him so much.

That kind of put a damper on our friendship, and we drifted apart over the years. I guess we never take into consideration that no one really wants to hear what you are going through if they are going through the same type of drama themselves.

So, you find the perfect man or woman for you and all you talk about is what people have done to you or how you don't feel loved. When I brought up these things and asked his opinion, he said, "When a man tells you that you look good, you don't believe it." So, he posed a question to me, "How do you know if I or any other man is actually honest about you being the only one they are seeing?"

I responded, "anyone that's been in a serious relationship and shared the same roommate and bed with their spouse, or significant other has had more than me." He laughed.

Another guy I stopped and asked said that he was so into this girl, then she started bragging about what she/her family had. He said it was a big turn off because he felt as though he would never be able to please her. Her expectations would be too high, and he couldn't afford her.

Sometimes it might be better to let a person find out on their own what you and your family have. What you think is a lot may only be a little to him.

Yet, another thing a woman could say to help end her relationship is talk about her expenses. A good friend of mine is such a diva, but she always asks me why she can't seem to hold on to a man? My reply was "you're always talking about your bills and what you cannot pay or need money for." A man will run fast if he thinks you're a gold digger. You should take care of yourself and your bills. Never go into a relationship with financial problems. On occasion, ask him out to lunch and/or dinner.

This not only impresses him but shows him that you're not afraid to take care of expenses and treat him for a change. Some men are not used to a woman being in control or buying them things. Show them that what little bit you have can turn into a lot if you work together.

Do this. Make a list of some of the things you would like to accomplish in a relationship. For instance:

- *Security* —Letting him know that you can take care of yourself.

- *Confidence*—Believing in yourself. By doing this, you show that you can stand on your own two feet and not rely on others.

- *Time Management*—Being able to acquire what you want, when you want it, and still take care of your significant other.

- ***Silence***—Knowing when to listen than to speak. A talkative person is a definite turnoff. I should be aware that by now. LOL.

As you know, the list can go on but these four things: ***confidence*** in yourself, ***security*** of taking care of yourself, being able to ***manage your time***, and knowing when to keep ***silent*** is vital to a relationship and will help you to access where you stand in the process.

No one wants to be told that they are dull, elusive, or carry too much baggage. This can damage a relationship and even the person you are speaking too.

Be true to yourself and the one you love. What you bring to the table could make for a never-ending feast of happiness.

CHAPTER TWENTY-ONE

A Day of Craziness

Ever felt like you are under too much pressure when hubbies around? You wish he'd go way or out of town for a few days? Ever hide money in a private account from a spouse because mom always told you to have your own nest egg? How about bribing him with favors to get what you want?

Now, let's take it one question at a time and try to compound them all into one.

You've been so busy trying to please your spouse, and he just seemed to get on your last nerve. No matter what you do around the house, he gripes. So, you come up with a plan to help the both of you. You suggest he takes a trip out of town to see his parents that he hasn't seen in over a year. He tells you he's busy, but you insist he needs a vacation. He finally caves and gives in. You're overjoyed so much that when he leaves, you run through the house without any clothes on just to see how it feels.

Yes, I do it all the time. I used to look forward to my husband and boys going to Tennessee. As soon as they'd leave,

I'd take long sudsy baths and run throughout the house jumping and screaming without anything on. Then, I burst into laughter enjoying peace.

Next, I'd go shopping. Since I have a secret account, I'd go and buy any and everything I want because it was my hard-earned money. Afterward, I'd take myself out to dinner or lunch—depends on the time of day.

Then when they come back home, you find another reason for him to leave. Or better yet, you tell them that you have a book signing in Virginia or South Carolina just so you can get away. Not that I didn't love my family, but there are times when you just want to be alone and write. You made a promise to do something extra special for them when you come back.

But when you return, he's already gone to the mall and bought you a diamond bracelet. You make every excuse as to why you're too tired to uphold your promise but will get together with him soon.

~

Ladies, I'll pause for a moment. Most men and women would have gotten a little suspicious of you if you've made promises after promises, but you don't keep them. If you're out doing something you're not supposed to with someone else, eventually you're gonna get caught. Stop making excuses and uphold your wedding vows.

~

Now he's angry at you and promises not to buy you anything else until you fulfill the promises you made to him and the family. You look at him and tell him, okay he wins. He smiles and says, "It better be worth it."

You wince, and you're mad because he's not letting you out of his sight. Your kids are hungry, and you have too many things to do to keep him company.

So, here's what you do. You say, "Well I guess momma didn't uphold her promises like she thought she had. But I'm tired, and the next time, I will be with you longer. How about a rain check?" Then, you give him that sad somber look and walk away. He'll probably chase you and beg for forgiveness.

The next day, you saw something in Macy's that you just had to have. You give him a call, but he's unreachable. You keep dialing him, and you get a busy signal. You must make a decision and decide to place the item on his credit card. It may sound greedy, but it might discourage him from wanting favors from you all the time.

I mean—come on already. Women get tired of having to beg their man for something nice. It shouldn't always have to be tic for tac. It's your wife, and she is your Queen. They don't realize all the things a virtuous woman does to keep them happy. Being a nine to five woman, watching the kids afterward, cooking dinner, cleaning the house, and washing clothes is a lot for one person. If husbands contributed, wives wouldn't have to bribe or beg for gifts of kindness.

It should be a given. Besides, where are the important things like the hidden money and bank accounts?

Chapter Twenty-Two

Killing Me Softly

Have you ever had that special someone from long ago that just won't go away? Okay, I'm talking twenty plus years, and you still can't seem to shake him or her. You hadn't seen or heard from em' in over fifteen years, but not a day goes by that you couldn't get em' off your mind. Whether it was his six pack abs or her curvy hips, his silky skin or her long hair, those luring eyes, or the way you were held, the memories just won't go away. I'm sure all of us probably have someone whether male or female in our life that's unforgettable and in essence is killing us softly. You want more than anything to be with that person, but then you reminisce and think about those twenty something years. Now, you remember why the breakup.

It could've been many things just to name a few:

1. Long nights staring out the window waiting hours for that special someone to take you out but he or she never shows up;

2. Always had an excuse for being late;

3. Why he or she couldn't come over;
4. You go over to his or her house, and another person is waiting to go on a date with the same person you are.

These are just a few things that can damage a relationship. I'm sure you might have others, but those were some of the things that kept us apart. On top of that, I decided to join the military and put my spy cap on. Bad…bad…bad idea. Joining the Navy was great. Just don't do it to follow someone. This man made such an impact on my life that I was willing to follow him to the ends of the Earth. Although he had negative tendencies, the positive ones outweighed them.

Like for instance: I recall our very first date. He took me to a restaurant in Scenic Heights in Pensacola, Florida. Back in 1988, the price for lunch was $12.95. My mouth flew open, and the next thing out of his mouth was, "if you're looking at the prices, please don't. I can't pay you enough for going out with me tonight."

Tell me those aren't the type words that will melt your heart. Then, to top it off, he took me on another outing at Pensacola Beach. He had gone by a rib joint and picked up some food: barbecue ribs, coleslaw, baked beans, and all the fixings. He had it all planned. He wouldn't let me get out of the car until he had everything laid out. He put a blanket on the ground. Then, he came back for me. This man picked me up and carried me over to the blanket. He said, "a beautiful woman like you should never have to put her feet on a ground like this." Talk about your great romances. Again, he was killing me softly with his words and actions. He knew how to win my heart and break it at the same time.

But sometimes, even good times must come to an end. My first ex-husband was coming back from Advanced Individual Training (AIT). Yeah, I cheated. But that's another story. We met in downtown Pensacola at Seville Square. He wrote the most amazing thing on a piece of napkin that took my heart away. It said, "Only once in a lifetime, if you're lucky. You find that special person, and they make your dreams come true. You have been a dream to me, and I only wish that you live 1 million years and I live 1 million years less one day so that I may never know a day without you in my life."

Come on ladies. Tell me he isn't worth giving him access back into your life? Right? Wrong! Those were special times. The bad outweighed the good moments. I tend to live in the past, and it seems I can't get my future right from dwelling on the past. Hey, I'm only human. *Sometimes, too human.* I dwell on incidents that took place long ago and hold a grudge because of them. God help me! I believe that is why things didn't work out with my recent ex-husband. Things that happened with his sisters and mother, I dwelled on and wouldn't let go. I let it ruin what we had.

Ladies and gentlemen, if you're reading this also, *let go.* If we continue to dwell on what should've, would've, could've been, then you'll never enjoy the future. Yes, he killed me softly with his words and actions, and quite frankly, I had problems getting over him.

I tell myself day in and day out that I won't answer the phone if he calls. I won't respond to his text messages, and I am going to change my cell number. The reality, I responded to his calls because he had a voice that made my insides move and my heart melt. I'd wait days before I answered his text messages and I changed my phone number but got upset one day with my current friend and sent him a text. That gave him my phone number all over again. I guess it's like the song says, "I can't get over you. I tried, and I tried, I just can't get you off my mind." I'm going through life changes, and I need his ear. Amazingly, he always knew what to say to make me feel better. But of course, he did. That man held my heart in the palm of his hands.

Problem: I've fallen in love with another man that looks just like him. How ironic is that? What are the odds of that happening? With him, I don't have to worry about not being loved, waiting for hours for a date, or another woman outside his door. *Ain't God good!*

Solution: Leave the past where it is! The past! Your future could be staring you in the face. However, if you continue to let the past stay in the present, your future would be nothing more than a *Killing Me Softly* song on repeat!

CHAPTER TWENTY-THREE

Ten's A Crowd and One Loudmouth Too Many

JUNE 19, 2010

Ever *asked, yourself 'Why'?* What possessed me? And, who made you the freakin' boss? Now imagine! Your dream vacation—nothing but you, three thousand people from different nationalities, a few spoiled kids, and one loudmouth reject God had pity on. I was all ready for my vacation trying to celebrate my freedom from being married for over nineteen years. When we got to the rendezvous site on time, we had to wait for the others to arrive. We were supposed to leave at nine, but because people are human and cannot seem to tell time or can't find the meeting point, we ended up leaving an hour and a half later.

Then, it happened. I was instructed to ride in an Escalade, but I insisted on riding in a crowded van with my newest friend and his daughter. I met all these people I had never seen before and one loudmouth who ruined my entire trip. For eleven hours, I heard about her chronic disease and how she had beaten it. I started to tune in because by now everyone else has to tune out. I felt awful for her and stayed attentive. Then, I made a comment about being gone for six hours and still haven't left Georgia. She had the audacity to say, "Just relax and go with the flow."

"Relax? Go with the Flow? *Girl, stop!*" I said snobbishly. "We were supposed to leave at nine, and be there by four? It's after eight and we've just arrived."

Everyone is tired, and the sweetest two-year-old little girl I ever met is on vacation with me. I went to pick her up to give her grandmother a rest, but the loudmouth woman belted. I paused because I didn't know what to think. Her husband who invited us to the cruise through his niece told her it was okay. I didn't know what to expect as we took this long journey to nowhere. I just tried to engage in a conversation only to find that the loudmouth was taking over.

By now, I just want to go to my room and relax. Getting through customs was hectic. You had to have the right documents and know where you were going. Finally, we reached the elevator and my friend, and his daughter was on the opposite side of the ship. *Dang!* This was going to be rough. *TIC TOC* and time has dwindled away on my first day of vacation. When I arrived at the elevator with most of the people in the van, all kinds of mess broke loose. *Time is ticking away!*

That cute little girl that I've been helping the entire trip reached for me. I started to smile and reached back. Then, I heard this loud scream, "Don't touch her! If I tell you not to touch her, then don't touch her." About 15 people are standing there watching this woman make a jackass out of herself.

"But she's my friend," the little girl said.

My heart dropped, and without thinking again, I reached out for her.

This woman yelled again, "I said don't touch her. If you don't tell her to stop, then I will," she looked at her husband. By now, everyone was staring at me as though I was a child predator. I didn't know what to do. I didn't want to stoop to her level, but I wasn't going to let her humiliate me either. I was utterly baffled. Instead, I got on the elevator and didn't say a word to anyone.

We got to the room, and one of her friends was in the room with me. So I asked her, "What is her problem other than cancer?"

"Well," she said. "You know that he is her husband."

'Okay, Freeze frame!' Did I miss something because I thought this was about a cute two-year-old baby girl? Now, I'm

really confused. "What do you mean by he is her husband?" I asked.

"Well you know she has cancer, and very protective of her husband."

"First of all," I snarled. "Her husband is nowhere near my type. Secondly, I was merely offering my help."

"Well, I think she felt threatened."

"Whatever!" I stated. "I will keep my distance." I stormed out the room. I managed to find my friend and his daughter and enlightened them. He expressed empathy for me and said I did the right thing.

By now, my feelings and integrity were hurt. My dream vacation is now just a dream.

Cruisin' to Disaster
Day one . . . June 19, 2010

Quietly, I sat on the balcony of the 8th floor listening to the smashing waves pounding roughly against the walls of the Carnival Dream. The crescent moonlight shone in brightly atop the roof the rapidly moving dark sky and I wondered what or who brought me to the point of wanting to end it all.

Sudden spurts of a dive into the rushing waves rushed through my raging mind. Yet, I wondered why so much pain. I can't help the way I look. God blessed me to be fruitful and beautiful. I can't find peace, only emptiness in a world so cold and bitter. My heart cries. My soul is boggled. Why do they *hate* on me so much?

Dinner with the captain was supposed to be enjoyable. Pain-free. Yet, another night I allowed the loudmouth woman to get next to me. The feeling of not being wanted; not being a part of the group damaged my integrity.

The one I loved could not be with me. He was not there to share my tears and pain. But I know if he could have he would. So, I sat in an empty chair isolated from an enjoyable time, staring at the glass-walled in front of me. My mind pondering over what could be a terrible death at sea or a sparkling disco on the promenade deck where laughter and enjoyment are hailed by all. My eyes were red from the tears I shed. My heart pounded with defeat. My body was aching and tired from a long walk on Bay Street, and the hike to the hotel Atlantis Paradise Island.

Evil faces appeared across the sky laughing at me wanting me to give up or give into the torturous '*Witch*' that's on my vacation of a lifetime. I choose life, family, and happiness above all. God created me out of love not to be spiteful or lose hope, but to endure the bad things that come my way. I'm a joyful person. I'm a beautiful black female created in God's image. With time, I too, will be able to overcome the evil lurking in my head.

The Exposure of Blubber
Day two . . . June 20, 2010

The morning started with a sudden knock on my cabin door, and my roommate opened it. I was lying in my small twin size bed not suited for a child. Standing in my doorway was my dream, my hope, my ambition gazing brightly before me. My eyes were full of laughter. I knew something was special about him the day our eyes first met.

We engaged in an early morning breakfast before leaving for our tour to the Bahamas waterfront. I was determined to make this a fantastic voyage. The food was plentiful. Twenty-four seven. I'm sure many people will gain at least ten pounds or more on this seven-day trip to the rushing seas. I, for one, have met my challenge. So much chicken, shrimp, lobster, hamburgers, and hot dogs. There was Mexican, Thai, Caribbean, American, Latin American food—you name it. It's here. Vanilla, Chocolate, and Strawberry ice cream along with desserts of all sorts for days. Wow! I see why there is a scare of overweight people populating the nation.

We left for our tour at 10:30 a.m. embracing the blazing sun enveloping our bodies. Thousands of us hurried across the pathway looking for the sales of diamonds, liquors, and clothes we so richly heard about. Our guide tour rushed our aching feet, searching for half-price alcohol sales while I engaged in T-shirts and woven bags. We visited 'Effy,' a bargain diamond store promising to give a free necklace with the purchase of studded earrings.

After returning to our ship, I headed back to my cabin, only to find my oversized roommate sitting in her birthday suit! I was literally blinded by the sight of her. She commenced to engage in a conversation, and I stopped her short of saying, "I was just bringing my things back and getting ready for the captain's dinner." She didn't think I'd make it back in time, but I did, and I wish to God I hadn't after seeing her butt naked.

Why do people assume that just because you're the same sex, it's okay to expose themselves in front others? What if that person was gay or lesbian? What type of upbringing do people like that have? It's not okay, especially if you're well over 300 pounds and got bags hanging from all sides of your body. I know some people feel like just because it's your child or relative, it's okay to undress in front of them. It's not a carefree world.

Everyone ranted about the video where the woman thought it to be fine to take off her clothes while walking down the street. What does that say about her as an individual, a woman, if she's even that? She didn't consider the fact that strangers or children were watching her, but if a man grabbed her into an alley and raped her, he would be at fault.

Decency is everything people. We are well-informed, well-educated people that should know better. You have to remember what your children see you do today, might hurt their chance for growth tomorrow.

Though reality tends to prove that what may have seemed to be a great deal, the idea of getting something for free turned out to be more fictional than realistic. When we arrived to find these Arabian princes standing before us pleading their case for world-famous Gemstones, a light tunneled through my mind— "It's a ploy to get you to the store with the free fake necklace, then try and persuade you to purchase Topaz Gems worth more than your paycheck."

We left store after store without a Gem and headed back to the Carnival Dream. Many of the stones on board the *Dream* were cheaper than what we found on the outside.

I made my way to the bar and then to the casino where my luck just seems to run out. I mean—if I could just hear one jingle from the slot machine, I would have jumped for joy. I couldn't seem to score a quarter, though many that traveled with me found exceeding joy in hearing the bells ring.

I hooked up with two of the individuals I traveled with and went for a bite to eat. Later that evening, they both were struck with illnesses and returned to their cabins leaving me vulnerable to alcoholic beverages and rushing waves. A part of me wished I hadn't spent so much time away from my family in Georgia. While another part was glad I took the time to find myself. The *bargain* I thought I would get, didn't add up to the tragedies I encountered during my so-called dream vacation.

Day three

Frustration is starting to get the best of me. I'm so tired of feeling the waves. I've been cruising for almost four full days, and I'm about to go ballistic. I want to be loved so bad that I'm eating hot dogs at 1:30 a.m. to compensate for it. I mean…this was supposed to be my vacation of a lifetime, but I can't seem to have things go my way. I've gambled at the casino so much that I'm starting to hear my dead mother's voice whispering, "Go back to your cabin" in my ears.

Why is it that some people have all the luck? It seems like they can have their cake, nibble, bite, and eat it at the same time. But I must smell the thing from a distance. I just cannot seem to get it right.

I caught this great deal—so I thought. Everyone, even the cute little two-year-old gets a $50 certificate/voucher back to spend on the cruise except for guess who—yep, me. I got a lot of headaches thinking about it.

To top it off, those backstabbing sons of a biscuit eaters are laughing in my face. If bad luck wasn't my friend, I didn't know it. I spent the entire day with the man I care about, only to go to bed lonely and wanton because he and his twenty-something-year-old daughters are sharing a room together. Talk about being irritated to the high heavens!

I'm a woman of passion, and I can't even get… Gheeze! Give me a break! What the heck is going on here?

Now I'm sure many men would love to enjoy my love, but my eyes are set, focused, and belong to a man who told a jeweler on June 21, 2010 "I was his better half." I couldn't wait to clarify this but what's a better half if you can't get close to him?

So once again, I sit around the pool surrounded by at least twenty teenagers and a bunch of disco dancing drunks watching the waves beneath me. A million thoughts rummage through my unsatisfied mind, pondering over what tomorrow will bring if God allows me to live through tonight. Life is hard, lonely, and challenging. I thought greener pastures would be on the other side, but I guess I was wrong.

Day four

The day started out in a frenzy. I awakened at 7:00 a.m., and our ship was to dock at eight. I hurried along after receiving a call to meet up in the Lido Lounge, an area where breakfast was being served. I arrived at approximately 8:10 a.m., scarfed down a croissant, some low-fat milk, and ran to the dock. Somehow, I thought the tour started at 8:30 a.m. No one in sight but me. Finally, I realized the tour started at 9:30 a.m. How nerve racking?

Now I sit alone once again in a cabin room not quite the size of an average hotel asking myself, "how did I get here?" I can't seem to find what I was searching for on this cruise. Nothing but loneliness and depression. I thought after getting divorced life would be peaceful. But I've come to realize that life for what I knew it, was not so bad. Well, maybe.

I wanted something different—more exciting! Frankly, I'm coming to realize that life is just what it seems—a rude awakening. But then again, life is what you make it, and *I* need to create a moment worth remembering.

As I continue on this cruise ship, rain was pouring all around us. I'm beginning to understand that being a victim of circumstance, loneliness, depression, and heartbreaks are all rolled up in one. This was not how it was supposed to be. I intended to be happy, having the time of my life and breaking free from life changes.

So, what's this loneliness all about? Is it a time when you feel like no one really cares about you? Or, is it when you need some time to yourself? Sometimes, we must ask ourselves if what we require is what we are actually seeking.

Here are some of the things I thought caused my disappointment while I traveled these blue seas:

1. Wanting something I couldn't have;

2. Thinking I was going to be with someone, and he was with his daughters;

3. Separating myself from the crowd I came with;

4. Finding out that I was going to sleep in a separate room from the one I loved for seven days.

So, what could I have done to not fall back into victim mentality?

1. First and far most, I should have checked ahead of time on the sleeping arrangements;

2. Made sure it was understood that this cruise was supposed to be for two not four;

3. Sought out different avenues before going on the cruise.

These were some of the things that I could have done, but you may think I could have done something else. In any instance, make sure you know what you are getting into before going into a situation, that way you won't be frustrated when things out of your control happen.

I remembered a song years ago, *Why Have I Lost You?* It talked about loneliness, and sometimes it can make you feel like you're on top of the world. That part I didn't understand because being lonely won't make you feel that way. It can make you want to be out of this world.

Day five
June 25, 2010, . . . Last Straw

What the freaking flying colors is going on? It's my last day to sleep in from five horrible days. I returned to my cabin in hopes of my roomie being asleep only to find her halfway dosed watching Oprah. It's the first-year anniversary of Michael Jackson's death, and Oprah remembers him. The problem is it's 3:30 a.m. in the morning and I'm tired.

I just finished washing clothes that cost $7.25 a load. Yes, $3.00 to wash, $3.00 to dry, and $1.25 for the smallest box of detergent. *Ooops!* Don't forget $1.25 for fabric softener. What a rip-off!

So here I am changing my clothes in the bathroom because this morbidly obese woman had the nerve to play, "Let's expose the chest" every chance she gets. I mean, C'mon! How many times do I have to watch her sitting there trying to engage in a conversation with her breast exposed and tent size underwear? I was utterly blindsided by the sight of them.

I came on this cruise in hopes of finally finding Donna Brown, but I found pain, misery, and seven exasperating days of sadness. So here we go. I'm sleeping, swore I wasn't getting up until 11:00 a.m. or so. Suddenly I hear, "I want my Dada." What was that? It's the cute two-year-old that I wasn't allowed to say anything to.

It's 8:45 a.m. and is not the time for me to get up yet. Then, five minutes later, I hear bags crumbling and things being tossed around the room. My roommate decides for me that it's time to wake up. So I say, "What's up with the noise?" Hoping she gets the message that I'm trying to sleep.

"Oh, I was opening up my bag!" *Who gives a flying dragon in China…I'm trying to sleep…is, what I'm thinking.* The bag rattling continues and instead of finding Donna Brown, I've found Portuguese—the alter ego I used to write my romance novels like, *Excuse Me Miss But I'm in Love with Your Husband* and *That Woman's House.*

Now I'm upset. No sleeping in. No more sweet dreams. No more anything. I jumped out of bed, used the bathroom, showered, and put on the wrong robe hanging on the back of the door. This woman's scent is all over me now. Ewe! I'm so frustrated now. I'm trying to calm down, but if one more thing happens, it's a wrap! Jesus, keep me near the cross.

~

Okay ladies and gentlemen, now that you've read what I went through during my cruise, here's a test you need and should consider. Think about the things that bother you the most and things that encourage you. Now do this:

Make a list of positive and negative obstacles keeping you from succeeding:

1. Dig deep and find any jealousy streaks and get rid of them; Are you temperamental? Ask yourself why and what bothers you more?

2. How often do you smile? Compliment someone?

3. Do you live in the past? Can't seem to let an old boyfriend or girlfriend go?

4. Do you use the word 'yes' more than 'no'?

5. Do you treat yourself out to dinner, lunch, a new dress, or pair of pants?

6. Do you allow other people to control your path?

7. Do you suffer from stress, depression, or low self-esteem?

8. Are you in love with the wrong man or woman?

9. Do you suffer from different personalities?
    a. Born one way but live the way society wants you to live.
    b. Use a different name and blame your bad traits on that person.

If you can be honest with yourself and answered these questions truthfully, then you are normal. I challenge each of you to find yourself. I allowed people from husbands, family, children, and boss to dictate my life. But I forgot who I was.

I always blamed Portuguese or characters from my books… Roxie, or Chantal for my behavior instead of taking the time to find the person I was born to be.

I dare you to say, "No I'm not doing it this time" and say, "You do it." I'm going shopping. Take a trip without the family if possible. That's only if you have a child or children that are older than twelve. Whatever you do ladies, don't leave your young daughters with friends or relatives or a fiancé that has males in the house. You would be amazed what could happen to them while you're away.

You say, "You have to trust somebody sometimes." Would you rather depend on the unknown, than listen to your heart? Ever wonder why your significant other is so friendly with your little girl or teenage daughter? Wake up, ladies! You have probably been there, don't let your daughters go through what you went through.

I had to deal with that ever since I was six years old. Can you imagine your five or six-year-old little girl being fondled her whole adolescent years? Her mind is not apt to cope with such a violation. And for God's sake ladies, don't allow your daughters to walk around the house in a long T-shirt with no shorts. Men will be men, and they prey on innocent little girls, even if it's their own. Sound sick, right…lust is a beast! Even *daddy* will bribe them with candy or money and tell them you will believe him over them.

Teach your kids/daughters how to come to you. And make sure they know you will believe them. Don't let your child/children suffer like I did. It took years of trying to block out the men and women that molested and raped me when I was growing up including close family and friends. Don't make your child feel like he/she brought it on themselves or make them feel dirty.

Raise your sons and daughters to respect themselves and others if possible. If possible, talk to your significant other about walking around in front of your daughters and sons with boxers or a short gown without a house coat on. After all, they're not daddy's little girls or dare I say, little boys for no reasons. Sometimes, it may come with a price. Don't let that price be fondling or lusting over your offspring in less than a caring way.

This is a test of strength. See if you have courage to stand up for yourself and those you love. If you don't, who will?

Chapter Twenty-Four

My Reasons for Living

Every *day is another* blessing that God decided to keep me upon this Earth. Am I worthy? No. Do I appreciate what God has given me? You betcha! Furthermore, there are some things/people that God placed upon this Earth that I can't help but praise him for.

In the spring of 1991 on a quiet chilly day in Baltimore, Maryland, I found myself praying and begging God for a child. I felt like—if anyone deserved to be a mother, it had to be me. I mean...C'mon people were killing their kids, beating the snot out of them, and leaving them without food to eat. But I was a loving, caring person wanting to have someone in my life that I could nurture day in and day out. I literally was begging God to be a mother. Be very careful what you ask God for. He just might give it to you.

So there I was, twenty-five, married, and in the Navy. My husband at the time was still stationed at Fort Devens, Massachusetts and I was at Fort Meade, Maryland. I had traveled to see him on the 4th of July four weeks prior and drank a bottle of Very Berry Wine Cooler while we were having a little fun. Finally, able to relax and let myself go, I exhaled.

Then, one lonely night around midnight while in the Navy barracks, I jumped from my metal bed pouring in sweat, ripping my clothes off, and sitting on the toilet begging God to take the pain away. What could I have done to deserve such suffering? Yeah! I asked God for a child. And, He gave him to me.

For the past twenty-four years, I've nurtured, loved, clothed, wiped his snotty nose, administered medicines, spoiled, and advised him, just to give him up to the world. But would I trade him for another? Not in a million years. My son has given me so many reasons to live: his mere presence, laughter, and smartness. I couldn't ask for a better older child.

Yeah, he's stubborn, arrogant, and downright rude sometimes. But he wouldn't be my son, a (Wright) if he wasn't those things. However, Stevie is intelligent, witty, handsome, and daddy's boy. Then, came another. I decided in 1997, I wanted another child. It had been almost six years since my first, and he was getting very lonely. I couldn't give him another sibling because we had been in the country of Panama, and I refused to have a baby outside the U.S. I realized I was pregnant the same way I discovered with my first son. I was pouring in sweat. But this time, I knew what to do. I couldn't take my clothes off fast enough. I was smiling so widely I almost fainted.

The next day, I bought a pregnancy test and *made* the purple line be there. It was barely visible, but it was there! I was so excited but needed confirmation before telling anyone.

The doctor confirmed it. I was three weeks pregnant. I wanted a little girl so much, but I got confirmation—it was indeed another boy. *'Dang, I thought.'* No more tries for me. I asked God for two children—preferably a boy and a girl. But at that moment, I'd take whatever God had to offer. You see, sometimes we should be specific when we ask God for things.

I didn't get my little girl, but I got the best gift God could have given me, Darius. What a joy to have! He is everything a mother could ask for. He's charming, polite, witty at times, and very courteous. However, Darius has traits Stevie doesn't. He can calculate in his head. Like Stevie, he can be stubborn, and he has a serious attitude when rubbed the wrong way. In 2005, I found out that Darius has Autism. But he has the kind that made him brilliant…Aspber's Syndrome. Though he has his faults, he would never be traded for nothing in the world.

My children have always been my reasons for living and have given me the will to live when my world was caving in.

Chapter Twenty-Five

Gold Digging Women

Classifications of a Gold Digger

Do *Gold diggers have* a color? Recently, I spoke with several men and women about women and what culture is depicted more often as a *Gold Digger*. The conversation it struck was appalling.

My Question:

What culture of women is more susceptible to becoming a *Gold Digger,* "African-American, Caucasian, Hispanic, or Asian?" This lead to a five-hour conversation at one job and an hour conversation at another.

One guy said without a doubt African-American women. Of course, he was African-American. Another said, Hispanic. But amazingly, they all tend to agree that very few Asian women would fit this category.

I asked: What would make you think Asian women are not *Gold Diggers*?

His response was because most tend to stick to their own culture.

Not a realistic reply.

My logic was this: how many times have you seen an American G.I. go over to Korea and come back married to a Korean woman? Asian women, in my opinion, are prone to be *Gold Diggers* because they are brought up to gain and conquer the world at a young age. They send their young daughters to the streets as early as nine-years-old teaching them how to attract men. They trained them to do whatever it takes to make a man happy.

When a lonely G.I. (that is—a man that can't seem to score a woman in the United States) goes to Korea or any other foreign country, he can come back married and happy until the woman is Americanized. Once she gets to America and meets a more confident man, she will most likely dump him and seek greener pastures.

However, Asian women are not the only *Gold Diggers* out there. Another class of women to consider is African-American women. Their approach to getting what they want is a little different than the others. The younger generation is all about voice instead of power. They want their hair, nails, and toes perfect. They may come to you hard and harsh.

Here's how they do it:

Female—I need some money so I can get my hair, nails, and toes done.

Male—I just gave you money last week to get your nails, hair, and toes done.

That is the wrong way to approach a man if you want to look good. Let's try again.

Female—Honey, you remember that show I was telling you about? Well, it's tomorrow. My hair is not in the best of shape, and my nails look horrible. Can you help?

Male—Sure thing. How much do you need?

Bam! Just that fast you've dug into his pockets, and he never knew what hit him.

Asian and African-American women have their approach, but the cleverest of them all is Caucasian women *in my opinion.* Here's how they do it and men are left blindsided because they never knew what hit them. More often in the 21st century, we find African-American men reaching out to Caucasian women because they were told that they are more subtle and easy to get along with. But we hear that they are the most *gold digging* women in America. Studies show that out of all women living in the United States, Caucasian women work less and stay at home more. They are taught from birth to stay at home and let the man take care of them. They appear to be plain, but all along they fake who they really are.

Black men are looking for one thing in a woman. Peace. As we know, Caucasian women will appear to be Christian bound homemakers. However, they are digging deeply into the pockets of brothers and others that would have them. They hang around ballgames and hang out at NFL parties waiting for the opportunity to be approached, and just like that they have reeled in another wealthy black male. Their approach once they've accomplished their goal:

Female—She goes around chipped nails, split ends, or hair uncombed, dressing plainly and looking for sympathy.

Male—Come home from work and doesn't like the appearance of his woman. He says, "Sweetheart, here's a few dollars. Why don't you treat yourself to the hair salon and nail parlor? Also, buy a new outfit, because I want to take you out to dinner and show you off.

Female— "Really, but there's only one problem baby, I don't have any matching shoes."

Male—Digging in his pockets again, "Here's an extra $100. Go make yourself beautiful and make me proud."

Ka-Ching! And just like that, she's suckered another golfer, ballplayer, brother, etc.

Another class of women I've watched over the years are Latinos. Like Asian women, they tend to hang out around Army and Navy bases waiting for the opportunity to freedom.

I'll never forget when I was a contractor in the country of Panama. Beautiful women were everywhere.

However, every gate on Friday and Saturday nights had busloads of Panamanian and Columbian women waiting for the opportunity to head back to the states. Unfortunately, all it took was two dollars and a box of Popeye's Chicken, and the soldiers could have them for a couple hours. Sad, but true. Many Hispanic women lower their standards trying to get a good man that will help them get freedom from impoverished areas. But what does freedom cost them? A man that can give them what they want, or a guy that is overweight and dies of a heart attack a couple years later.

I spoke with a Caucasian male, let's call him Johnny, who's at least 310 pounds with thick glasses. He has been married six years. He was telling me about this woman that needed help and how he generously supported her financially, and eventually told her that since he was helping her out, they should get married. She agreed and now wants a divorce because she's unhappy. At the time, he was in the military, and she saw a free ride. However, after moving from California to Augusta, Georgia, she realized he wasn't what she wanted. Apparently, she thought him being a Caucasian male, he would always have money to take care of her.

Now that he's in the contractor world and not an E4 in the United States Army, she's an ecstatic twenty-four-year-old Asian woman. She can stay at home and not have to worry about the lack of things she doesn't have. So, now that I've taken you on an opinionated journey into the world of *Gold Diggers* can you honestly say African-American women are the biggest *Gold diggers?* I hope not.

So, who in your opinion do you feel are the biggest *Gold Diggers?* In my opinion, every culture has their fair share, but Caucasian and Asian women are a little more shrewd in the way that they approach and interact with the opposite sex.

CHAPTER TWENTY-SIX

Cheating

What makes a person cheat? Is it the lack of attention they receive at home or do they just get bored?

Sadly, over 40% of marriages end because of cheaters. Men say, 'women are too needy' or 'they argue too much.' Women say 'males don't hold up to their manly responsibilities such as taking care of the household, paying attention to them romantically, taking them out, etc.'

Is it okay to cheat? And, if so, when is a good time?

To answer any of these questions realistically, a person must already have their mind set on cheating. After being married for almost twenty years and getting divorced before the twentieth year, it crossed my mind several times. No matter how much I loved my ex-husband, the thought was always there. If he made me mad, I'd think about men from my past or present friends that would love to have a woman like me. The thing that would stop me was knowing I was married, my children, and my own low self-esteem about my body.

Having a man laugh at my body would have been devastating to me. I'm very paranoid about the stretch marks on my stomach and the varicose veins on both of my legs. In my eyes, men want a woman with beautiful legs, skin, and a flat stomach. I am very self-conscious about my body so I try and cover it as much as I can.

So, I asked some friends: Why they thought men and women cheat? Here are a few of their answers. I've used pseudonyms to protect the innocent, or maybe not, so innocent:

- It gives them power over their current situation—makes them feel superior to their mate.

- It's fun—says another. Nobody knows but you and the person you are with.

- Because the person they were cheating with was also married.

- They were unhappy with their current situation.

- There was no romance in their marriage.

So, is it easier for two married people to cheat than a single person with a married person?

"Of course," says Candy who's been married twelve years. I can have my cake, eat it, and if I don't like it, I can give it back without anyone knowing about it.

If the person you are cheating with is single, then their expectations are greater. They are looking for something in return other than fun."

"Everyone's doing it," Monty laughed. "I don't know one man single or married that hasn't stepped out. My father stepped out on my mother, and they are still married after thirty-two years.

"I got bored with my husband," Precious said. "After a while, we just turned away from each other at night, and he'd kiss me on the forehead. It was like I was his child or something. At least when I cheated, I know that person wanted me even though they couldn't have me."

~

I was appalled hearing the comments to my questions. So, is it okay to cheat? I posed the question again.

I wanted to answer this one myself. After sleeping in the room with my son for two years and then sleeping alone in another room for eight, I was so close but far away from cheating several times. However, I don't think it's ethical, nor biblical.

Exodus 20:17b says, "Thou shalt not covet thy neighbor's wife, nor his manservant, nor his maidservant,"

This is where the confusion therein lies. If you have been unhappy for years and had no intimacy with your spouse, then it's time to seek a counselor. You should not have to step outside of your household for happiness. You married that person for a reason. They caught your eye, and you fell in love. You should do whatever it takes to keep the fire burning. Again, why shouldn't you cheat? Because the Bible says so.

But what if all else has failed, and you feel like you're in a compromising situation? What is a person who catches your eyes and steals your heart? How do you release yourself from the situation?

We all know that life is short and we don't want to live our lives unhappy. Many have seen their mothers and fathers die without love. The mere possibility of going to your grave without anyone to love you or being loved has got to be the worst thing that could ever happen to a person.

God didn't place us on earth to be unhappy. He wants us to enjoy life and depend on Him for our heart's desires. God said it Himself. Just ask, and He will give it to us. But that doesn't give one the license to cheat.

Personally, when I was at the end of my marriage going through a divorce, vultures were everywhere. But I just wanted my freedom and to have peace for a change. I needed time to build my confidence and increase my self-esteem. Old lovers and others were on my back, but I thought about how my children would feel about me. The worst thing I could've done was introduce them to someone new without thinking about their feelings. I'm sure they would have ratted me out so fast to their father making me look like I left him for someone else. I trusted God, and He gave me the patience to wait for the right man that would appreciate me and love my children in the process.

~

So, while cheating may seem like a good idea, think about the consequences it may pose on your family:

1. Do you really want an incurable disease that you can't get rid of?

2. Would you like to lose the respect of your children, and gain the hate of your family?

3. Is it worth the risk of being caught and left degraded by your spouse?

Shasta says, "I don't think it's ever okay to cheat, but in some circumstances, I understand. If possible, talk it over with your spouse before engaging in a relationship with someone else. Ask them if they feel the marriage was worth saving?"

If you are truly unhappy in a relationship, cheating will only make it worse. For instance, most importantly, take some time to rediscover your marriage. Pamper yourself with a new hairdo, buy a new dress/outfit and go to a new restaurant.

One of the biggest problems overlooked in a marriage is a cheating spouse or accepting it. We hear R&B Artists singing about it, actors and actresses doing it, and your friends engaging in it. Some people habitually do it. It has become a natural way of life for them. Marriage is sacrificial and shouldn't be taken lightly...Do your best to uphold your wedding vows. Be honest with yourself and your spouse. If cheating is your way out, get help first, then experience life for what it is. Remember, it is never a good thing to cheat no matter what the circumstances are. Let's look into the life of Shanice, a fictional character from my book, *Secret Lies*.

Caught in a Lie . . . Shanice's Story

This *is like déjà vu* all over again. I'm sitting here on a flight heading to Virginia. Almost seven years ago, I was in the same predicament headed to South Carolina. I got on the plane back then, running late almost missing my flight. As I entered my seat, which was on the left side of the plane, two gentlemen late 50s and early 60s were seated next to me.

The difference back then, one was white (he was the older of the two) and sat in the aisle seat. The African-American gentleman, Ron, was sitting next to me. I was sad because my cousin had just passed and Ron politely got up so I could get in my seat. Sensing my demeanor, he struck up a conversation.

Fast forward to today, two African-American gentlemen sat next to me on a flight back to Georgia from Florida. They both appeared to be in their late 60s. They immediately struck up a conversation and had been talking since.

I'm sitting here holding my breath for dear life. *'Can someone please give the man next to me a breath mint?'* I thought to myself. I wasn't trying to be cruel, but his breath was so tart that it was burning my nose.

The entire flight we talked about golf, houses, and one of the guy's wives being the first African-American woman to graduate from Harvard. I believe Lambert was her name and she's been signing books for the past couple years.

"I'm enjoying my moments talking about these things, but nothing beats the memories of Ron," Shanice commented.

Ron is a classic. We've traveled together and met different times until a letter came addressed from him. My mail had come to my P.O. box, and I mistakenly mixed it up. Ron had sent me some beautiful cards to say hello, and he missed me. I accidentally left them in plain sight, and Frank found them. *Go figure! All these years of being sneaky and it came down to a misplaced letter.* A freakin' letter ruined my groove.

So clearly, I had to find a way to cover it up. I mean— that's who I am, a habitual liar, a deceiver, and an adulterous woman. It was clear that Ron even at his age had it going on.

~

Then, as I sat next to another guy flying home from Atlanta to Charlotte, I just knew he would catch a hint and notice me holding my breath for dear life. God help his wife! A breath saver is a key to holding a woman or a man. Eventually, I pulled out a pad and pen and started to write. Sometimes it's best to leave well enough alone and keep on truckin.

"So, you dabble a bit!" He said smiling my way.

'Excuse me,' I'm saying to myself as he interrupts my thoughts. I had to tell myself to hold my thoughts and compose yourself'! I heard my inner voice speak to me.

"Actually, I'm writing a friend of mine and telling her how much fun I had during my visit," I sharply replied hoping he'd leave me alone. But, he continued.

Ever wish you could travel back in time to a place where there's nothing but blue skies, warm weather, and tropical trees over the top of you while you're relaxed in a lounge chair sipping on a tall glass of your favorite drink?

Then the captain came over the airwaves, "It's a bit misty out with scattered clouds, but the sun will come out soon." Then he said, "We'll be arriving in Charlotte soon so relax and enjoy the ride."

The only ride I wanted at the time was to get my car and drive as far away from this guy as I possibly could. But no, I was stuck talking to *mister you need a breath mint, toothbrush, and scope wrapped in one.*

The plane couldn't land fast enough. I grabbed my bags and bid him farewell. Frank was waiting for me at the baggage claim area. He was a great sight to see. I wrapped my arms around him and told him how glad I was to see him.

We walked through the airport like we were the happiest couple in the world. We had our differences but always found a way to bounce back. I guessed mainly because he had lost one wife and didn't want to lose another. And, I understood that completely having lost my husband to HIV.

With that said, my heart hungered for Ron. He was so much fun to be around, and his conversations were always about how he felt about me. No matter how many times I tried to forget him, his name kept coming up.

"I've missed you so much," managing to squeeze out a terrible lie, pretending to still care. I knew I hadn't been entirely forthcoming of my whereabouts, but my options were limited at this point.

Frank wrapped his arms around me, then let go.

"Something wrong?" I nervously ask.

For a moment, he stood staring at me. "I love you so much, Shanice. I really want us to be a real family again."

I grimaced slightly and said, "I love you too Frank." We reached the car and headed down Route 77 until we reached our home. Frank guided me towards the living room where bits of roses and pansies were awaiting my return. I stood completely in awe, face covered, tears crowding my eyes. My heart was engulfed in deceit. *Why did he have to go there with me?*

"They're lovely Frank. I don't know what to say."

"Just say you will always love me and be honest."

'*He must know something,*' I thought.

I straightened my face and with the biggest lie ever told, I said, "Baby, I'm past that. Ron is a thing of the past."

"Good," then he said. "Show me. If you really love me, Shanice, show me and stop making excuses."

"Frank, I don't understand why you are acting like this all of a sudden. You know I love you. I continuously show you. I cook your dinner, wash your clothes, and clean your house. What else do you want from me?"

He shook his head. "I want your heart, Shanice. I want you to love me like you love Ron."

"Ron, why are you talking about him? I don't have feelings for Ron. He's not my husband Frank, you are."

Frank smirked. "You've never loved me, Shanice. I see it in your face. You can't even be honest with yourself."

"Frank…"

"Stop it, Shanice! I know you were with him. I had a tail put on you. I just had to see if you'd come clean. I want you to pack your bags and get out!"

"Frank please!" I begged.

"Get out Shanice! Maybe this Ron person will have you. I don't love you anymore."

All I could do was drop my head, tuck my tail, and head out the door. I can't believe I broke his heart like that.

Though this is a fictional story, many times in life, we forget the important things until they're gone. We think the grass will be greener on the other side until we lose what's precious to us.

Being faithful to yourself will help you to be honest with someone else in the end.

CHAPTER TWENTY-SEVEN

Unwanted Feelings

Have *you ever felt* unwelcome or like an outcast? Degraded, rejected or just lonely? How many times have you tried to fit in and was left as a laughingstock? If you've been through, or are going through any of these, you are not alone.

Many women and men go through similar situations. If negative emotions are left unresolved, mental, and physical issues soon surface: unnecessary stress, depression and poor job performance. Your relationship with your spouse, close friends, or people you encounter daily may also be affected.

We must realize that there is help whether psychological or spiritual. Many times, we face additional problems because we have a hard time expressing ourselves. Sometimes, what you meant to say came out wrong, and one slip of the tongue can tear a relationship—whether, intimate or friendly, apart. Finding ways to reconcile could be difficult.

I often think about the many relationships I've destroyed because I didn't know how to express myself or make myself clear. How many times have you been in a situation where you wanted to fit in, but there was always that someone holding you back. Terrified that you might say the wrong thing, you try and befriend a person for all the wrong reasons. For example, Popularity—you might not dress or wear your hair like the other person, but because you desperately want to be noticed or fit in, you try drastically to change who you are so that others might actually *see* you.

I reflect to a time when I wanted people to accept me, so I tried to be in their face as much as possible, or even tried acting their age. Actually, it made me look and feel immature, and insecure about who I am. It's important that when we try to be like others that we remember who we are.

Insecurity—making a fool out of yourself. This is my definition, not Webster's. When we look in the mirror and see the person looking back at us, sometimes we think:

- God, why isn't my face attractive?
- Ewe, that's a big pimple!
- Am I too fat or too skinny?

When will we look in the mirror and praise God for allowing us to be above ground? We are all made in God's image.

Celtics team—torn down to a point where you'd think everything about you is just plain ugly, that is my biggest pet peeve about myself. For instance—you came home and you had a great day, or not so good of a day at work. Or, you just went on a dream vacation and came back to tell it all. The first thing you hear is – you went looking like that? Did you even look in the mirror before you left the house? You've gained a lot of weight lately. Ever tried being on a diet?

Your day was just shot to the ground. Your sixteen-year-old just dropped to an all new low. Your head was topped with excitement just to have someone tear it to pieces.

Let's rewind for a moment. You wanted everyone to like you, but now you've somehow turned others against you. You feel insecure about yourself because someone called you names, or you had ugly pimples on your face. Possibly, you feel as if God just didn't do a good job when He created you! Now, you want to let go of any and everything that meant something to you.

So, what if people don't dig your style or you don't fit in. You should satisfy oneself first before trying to cater to others.

Recently, I ran into a person I knew years ago and thought hey maybe this person has changed over the years. So, what do I try and do? I introduce her to some people I thought I already knew and wanted there to be a big circle of friends. Guess what? It didn't work. It turned everyone I figured I had befriended against me, and she, in turn, gained their friendship.

My aunt told me years ago, "Donna—the person I'm still trying to find" you can't buy love or friendship. This came from the heart. Now the uneasy feelings or unwanted feelings come into play:

1. You're no longer focused on what you've tried to gain.
2. You've lost respect, self-control, and your so-called friends.
3. You're an outcast!

At this point:

1. You want to crawl under a rock and hibernate.
2. You want your remaining friends to steer clear because you break hearts or hurt feelings.

Remember! You are battered as well. You don't have to go at it alone. There is help, and the only way you can solve your problems is to seek it.

You're not the only one with hurt feelings. Many people share unwanted emotions. It's up to us to resolve them. So, what if it won't make you well-liked. It will give you peace of mind.

Research your steps and take control of your mind. Try to remember who you've talked to, who you told what, and how the event occurred. If you can find out this information, maybe the answer to your problem is a step away from being resolved. Take the time to choose your friends wisely and know who you can and cannot trust.

Remember, a slight slip of the tongue can destroy a relationship that you've built, in a matter of seconds. Take the time to know yourself before getting to know someone else.

CHAPTER TWENTY-EIGHT

Tied To Their Children

Many *times we think* the world revolves around us—you and I/him. Then you meet his genuine reason for living. There is a thing called '*daddy's girls*' and '*momma's boys,*' and I've met the epitome of the real daddy's girls.

I've come to realize that the love they share is pure but sometimes that love can be damaging. There are times when it's okay to communicate with your grown daughters or sons that you have a life, and have done your best to raise them, but it's time for them to venture out and discover the world on their own.

When you've made plans to be together for the evening, and your grown children interrupt with wanting to do something else or just sit and talk with you, it places a damper on your relationship. You sit and start taking note of what's going on. You realize that no matter what you do to try and please them, they will always have momma or daddy's heart.

So where do you fit in? Do you come before or after? Do you smile when they are around and exhale when they are not? Do you compete for his or her love, or do you try and share the little pieces that are left behind?

No, First and far most, you don't. If he or she has you in their life, it's because they want you there. Many people have a certain type of love for their children, and sometimes you think because they are grown, the parent will focus more on you and leave them behind. That's far from the truth. You must realize that they share a special bond with their children that you may not have. They've known each other since birth, and you could just be getting to know their father. You didn't live in the same house as they did. You weren't there in the wee hours of the night bathing them, wiping their noses, or drying tears from their eyes. You sure weren't there when they took their first step or said their first words. So why would you think you'd come first and them second? It doesn't matter how old they get, in momma or daddy's eyes, they will always be their children. Don't try and change who he or she is, or the relationship with their children. In the long run, you will lose.

So, how do you compete when you're the mother and your daughter dumps you for daddy? What if you did everything daddy did but your daughter seems to love her father more? Do you wonder about their relationship? Is it perverted if you even suggest they are too close?

Here is a question I have asked many women wanting to know how they felt about a situation. The responses were mind boggling.

"Would you allow your teen daughter to walk around the house in a T-shirt and underwear in front of their father? Honestly, I've had many different responses to this question.

One lady said, "If it doesn't bother the mother, and their household has an open relationship, then it shouldn't be a problem."

A response like that bothered me. If you allow your teen daughters especially if they *got back* as they would say, or have oversized breasts, Daddy will more than likely take note. He's a man, and his eyes will wander. He may be man enough to tell her to go put some clothes on, but nine times out of ten, he won't say anything because they are *'daddy's little girls.'*

I'll never forget when I was about eighteen and went over to my uncle's house. The bra I had on was very light weight and sheer. He immediately he asked, "Girl, do you have on a bra?" I appreciated that because my uncle instilled something in me, I hadn't encountered at my mother's house. By doing so, I could teach my boys how to present themselves in the presence of women while they were young. If you allow them to roam around any way they please, it only causes confusion when they get older. Teaching them at an early age instills morals and teaches them to take pride in who they are.

But, if the parents walk around in front of the children partially naked, how can a child learn what not to do if the parent is doing the exact same thing?

For instance, a five-year-old girl and a ten-year-old boy regularly see their mother in a see-through gown, and the father walks around in boxers with an exposed chest. By the time they reach puberty, they have been allowed to roam around likewise. Now, you have a situation. Not only is the father watching his daughter develop but so is the son.

The Bible teaches us to take pride in our bodies for our bodies are the temple of the Holy Spirit (1st Corinthians 6:19*a*). If it is exposed and entices people in your family, then the family secrecy is broken. A lot of people find nothing wrong with this because they have become accustomed to it. By the time a girl is wearing a training bra, she should be covered and take pride in herself. I've seen some families walking around with the top exposed and bottom covered only by a towel. I've also seen the father walking around topless in boxers, and the daughter who is old enough to drive, walk around in front of her father in her panties and a T-shirt with no bra on. I've seen a brother, sister, and girlfriend all stripped down to nothing taking a shower like they were crunched in a military shower with one shower head.

Tell me, where do you draw the line? Is that why there is so much incest in the families? Could that be the reason why so many fathers put their daughters ahead of anyone to include their own wives? Girls know they have a hold on their daddies, and I believe that is why it's so hard for them to give their daughters to another man. Fathers are very skeptical when it comes to their daughters. They protect them in every way possible.

The next time you see a little girl clinging to her father instead of her mother, just know that now is the time to break the bond. I'm not saying leave your daughters out to dry but teach them to respect themselves and most of all, respect you. Remember their body is the Lord's Temple and should not be defiled acts of lust.

Growing up, I considered myself or wanted to be a *daddy's girl* because I am his baby girl. What I got in return was a one-way ticket to madness and back. Though he had good intentions, my father wasn't the fatherly type. As much as I needed, wanted, and craved my dad's love, it wasn't there. My dad didn't know how to love because his father didn't set that example for him.

Until this day, I still crave my papa's love even though I'm forty-four. I know he loves me, but he just wasn't taught how to love. I guess that's why I get so envious of women and girls when I see them being loved by their father. I thank God I didn't follow my dad's footsteps. My boys know what it is to be loved, but they also know that exposure doesn't work in my household. They were taught at a very young age and until this very day what is proper. Neither one of them has seen me improperly dressed beyond the age of four.

Chapter Twenty-Nine

Incest

When a Father Loves Too Much

Let me take you on a journey that some of you may recognize. I'm very adamant about this because I've been in situations of abuse not by my father or uncles but by other people I've encountered while growing up. Hopefully, it will help you seek help before it's too late if it should ever happen to you or your child.

She found herself staring widely at the room and gold curtains hanging on her bedroom window. The door was halfway cracked, and the room darkened. Most of the sheets were dangling from her twin-size bed. The ceiling fan was slowly going around in circles as she watched him come towards her.

Tears welled up in the corner of her eyes as she brought her pale narrow knees to her chin. "Please not again," Kerry begged. But the alcohol on his breath reminded her that when

Daddy gets drunk, he doesn't hear her cries nor remember what he's done. The abuse started when she was eleven, and now at the age of twelve, her body had already begun to take the form of a young lady.

She closed her eyes and wished she was in a fantasy land when her Daddy came at her.

"You'd better not cry this time Princess," he smiled down at her. "You know how much Daddy loves his baby girl," he said. "Daddy is going to buy you a really nice gift after I get what I want."

Kerry sniffed quietly looking at him. She was afraid to interrupt him.

He raped her and cautiously got up from her bed wiping away her tears.

"Now cut that out, Princess. Daddy wouldn't be doing this to you had your momma not gotten so old. You were *real* good this time Princess. Remember, you can't tell nobody about this. They wouldn't think too kindly of us doing this, now would they?" He told her poking his lips out at her.

"No Sir," she said sadly dropping her head.

"Now you go back to sleep and Papa will see you around the same time tomorrow." He left the room closing the door behind him.

Sitting in a chair next to the mahogany dresser was his wife pouring in tears. Her husband was fastening his pants and looping his belt buckle. He gave his wife a snobbish smirk and told her to go fix him a sandwich. She rolled her big brown eyes at him and walked towards the kitchen. It was all she could do to stop herself from going back into her bedroom to take a nap before she whacks him with a skillet. Fifteen years of long tiresome pain she endured with him, and he continually rapes her daughter. She was tired of his mess. She knew it had to end or somebody was going to get killed. Preferably not her.

Three months later, she noticed a change in the way her daughter Kerry's clothes were fitting her. She covered her mouth. "God no! Please don't let my daughter be pregnant by that monster." Suspicion got the best of her as she took her to the doctor. True enough her daughter was pregnant with her husband's baby.

But how could she explain this? Would it make her daughter look cheap if the truth was told? Or, will her husband be charged with raping and impregnating his own daughter?

It wasn't long before everyone knew about her pregnancy. She could no longer conceal it. No one knew the specifics except the ones that lived in the household, and they were sworn to secrecy. After other family members had found out, they chased him out of town and vowed revenge. What type of man does this to his own daughter?

Ladies, listen very carefully! Although this is fictional, I have met several women that have told me similar stories to what you have just read. A couple of their fathers were ministers. I spoke about this earlier on, but when you allow your daughters to walk around the house half-naked and they have already started to physically develop, their fathers will take note. Please protect your daughters and show them as much love as possible so that they won't be a statistic.

CHAPTER THIRTY

D o you suffer from a type of love where you would do anything to keep the person you are seeing? Maybe if the opportunity presents itself '*kill?*' It's an active addiction that a lot of women more so than men suffer from. It's call '*mad love.*' No, it's not found in any dictionary or encyclopedia, but it resides daily in the minds of desperate women. Whispering voices telling them that they would do almost anything to keep him in their life. It's a sickness that if gone untreated could pose a serious or even a gravely threat to others.

One of the principal causes of this so-called '*mad love*' is an infatuation of being with a married man. Women who mess with married men allow themselves to think only of one thing—themselves. They don't care who gets hurt in the process, or how damaging it can be to someone else's marriage. Many women believe that somehow what they are doing is better than the man's wife and eventually, he will leave his wife for her.

However, very few, probably less than twenty percent will give up what they have at home. Men look at the *cost* of giving up on a relationship, rather than their own happiness. It's one of the reasons they cheat. Why release the cake when they can have it, and a slice of pie too? It's much easier for them to continue cheating and go home to misery instead of paying a lifetime for a divorce.

Women, on the other hand, will abandon their families quicker than a man if they're not happy. Women seek love, affection, and comfort. If any of these are missing, they will drop you like a hot potato and jet! When a woman wants something bad enough, there is no limit to her means of acquiring it.

For instance, let me take you on a journey a lot of women get caught up in and then find themselves depressed, desperate, and empty. Sit back, observe, enjoy, and take note.

She watched him daily in the corner of her powder blue eyes. His physique, humor, and intelligent being drove her wild. She was one rarely possessing a smile barely giving in to the comfort of a grin. Her self-esteem was low. Yet, Bob made her smile. Overwhelmed by his approach, Betty felt nobody understood her like Bob.

Betty lived by herself. No sight of a male existence in her world until Bob gave her a smile and felt compelled to engage in a conversation. Betty being shy and naive turned red.

Bob knew he had found an easy target. He wasn't happy at home but wasn't ready to end years of marriage for someone that didn't have the confidence to stand on her own.

Betty sat at her desk one day typing the same phrase over and over and over again. *What if he wasn't my boss?*

Bob came by and asked what she was doing after work, and would she like to have dinner with him?

Betty snickered covering her face. Just that fast, Bob had his prey. He had just baited his hook and reeled Betty in.

After dinner, he suggested they go and have a snack at her place. He wanted to be far away just in case someone saw him. After all, Betty wasn't the most beautiful woman he worked with, and if seen with her, he would be immediately interrogated. Betty didn't mind. She didn't even question him. She immediately said, "You know what Bob, that's an excellent idea."

They took her car leaving his at a park a couple of miles from her home. Smooth Bob moving swiftly, barely giving her the chance to open the door and pushing his way into her living room. Bashful Betty was taken aback dropping her head. She had an odd candid smile on her face and slowly raised her head up towards Bob.

"Would you like something to drink?" She asked, letting her dark brown hair down.

"I wanted to talk to you about something if it's alright with you."

Betty smiled. "What's this about?"

"Well," his phone started to ring. He shook his head. It was his wife. He cleared his throat and silenced her.

"Is there a problem?" She asked after he got off the phone.

"A slight one. Listen, I have to go now, but maybe we can pick this conversation up later."

"Are you sure you have to leave? I mean…you just got here."

"Yeah, maybe this wasn't such a good idea, me coming over here in the first place. I'll see you at work tomorrow, and we'll have some tea or coffee together at the Starbuck's around the corner." He leaned over and gave her a small peck on her cheek.

Betty started to blush. "Okay, I'll see you then."

"Oh, and Betty, you can't tell anyone about this. We can get into big trouble me being the CEO you know."

"Don't worry, Bob. I won't tell a soul." She opened the door, and they walked out. She had to take him back to get his car. On the way, back she couldn't get her mind off him.

Days later, Betty sat at work thinking about what could've happened if Bob hadn't received that phone call. She couldn't think of no one or nothing else but Bob. She doodled at work all day twisting the ends of her hair with her index finger. Doris, one of her senior coworkers, pulled Betty aside. She enlightened Betty about Bob status. She tried telling her about Bob being married. But Bashful Betty didn't look concerned. She figured since Bob had kissed her, he couldn't have been happy at home.

Betty started doodling again. This time she wrote, *'I wonder what would happen if his wife wasn't around.'* She smiled heavily and continued writing. A few minutes later, Bob came around the corner. She scurried fixing herself accordingly.

"Hello Betty," he spoke, then gave her a slight wink. Young, naïve, and Bashful Betty snickered. "Hi, Bob."

"How are you?" He asked.

She smiled widely. "Tired but excited about us."

Bob stood puzzled. "Betty, I think we need to talk." He paused. "I believe that you're a very sweet and beautiful young lady. Any man would love to have a woman like you but, well, Betty, to tell the truth, I'm a married man and you already knew that."

Betty smiled gingerly. "What if your wife wasn't a factor?"

Bob was appalled by her question. "Betty, I'm married. Maybe not happily, but I have no intentions of leaving my wife or family. We've only spent a short time together. You work for me. What are you, *crazy?*" He voice was crisp.

"But Bob—it was all in the way you kissed me. I know you care."

Silently, studying her… Bob replied angrily. "We're not having this conversation."

"Excuse me?" She grimaced.

Furious, Bob responded. "Forgive me Betty, but you have to forget I ever came over to your place. It was just an innocent peck on your cheek. I can't see how you got something romantic out of that. I think we need to talk about your position here at Turner Construction." He removed himself from her presence.

~

You see thousands of women facing what Betty was going through. Realistically, they are left dejected and shameful after messing around with someone else's husband. Many get so angry and do like Amy Fisher, but mostly accept defeat and move on.

Before you do something drastic, seek counseling or just leave. After talking to a male friend at work about this situation, I am compelled to say that the ball was hit right out of the ballpark.

According to him, he's been married for over twenty years and has worked with many women. He would never walk out of his marriage even if he had cheated. He felt like he could just as easily get what he wants at home but chooses to get it elsewhere.

He also mentioned that he's not sure if he even has feelings for his wife, but he does know that she was and is the only woman that could put up with him and put him to sleep at night.

So, there you have it, from a man that's been married for over twenty years and not sure if his love for his wife is genuine. He would never leave her for another woman. Why you ask? As the saying goes, *It's Cheaper to Keep Her*!

We can't be foolish thinking that a married man would give up the comfort of his home for someone else he barely knows. Someone else's husband is not right for you. Find someone that would be faithful to you and care for you only.

When I told him that I only allowed a man to touch me if I had feelings for them, he laughed and said, "Your problem is you're too needy. A man is looking for love, not a woman in need." He also stated that "they're looking for someone to comfort them until they can find someone else."

Find your own comfort zone and leave (TOW) the other woman's man alone. The audacity of him saying, comfort them until they can find someone else, bothered me.

I guess in the eyes of most the opposite sex, women are just a means of temporary satisfaction they can play with until they get bored and desire another toy.

CHAPTER THIRTY-ONE

Screaming Out Loud

Ever have one of those days where nothing seems to go right, and you want to run outside and *scream out loud?* Maybe it was the way you got out of bed that morning, the dog pooped on the floor, and your feet just happen to step on it. Or, you were running late for work—got in the garage, put everything in the car, and turned the light out—you tried to follow the regular outline of the car, but you took some medications for your hand; that, by the way, does absolutely nothing but knock you out. Then, you hurry around the back of the car and *Bam*, you hit your arm on the handle of the garage. You feel for blood hoping and praying you didn't rip a hole in your arm—asking for forgiveness and saying '*Halleluiah*' for another day. You back out real fast almost knocking the fence over around the garden and then you pause.

You figure you're still alive; you have your health. Things aren't as bad as they could be. Then you get to work, and your biggest fear is right in front of you—cockroaches. You dash for the door, and everyone is staring at you wondering what got into you. You walk in looking like a bag woman from another planet. Not to worry, though. The person you're relieving is already one step out the door before you can even get a full shift brief. A few weeks prior, she literally fell out the door trying to leave before her shift was over. So you check out everything to make sure it's okay, and you exhale.

Minutes later when things quiet down, you breathe, and a thought comes to your mind, "Oooh child, things are going to get easier. Oooh child, things are going to get brighter." This song originally came from a group I've never heard of called *'Stair Step Five,'* but I'm glad they made the song.

Often, we want to *'scream out loud'* when our day is going bad, or lose a family member, or even when you make a bad decision and can't recant it. When I sat in the tub last night listening to beautiful sounds taking place in my house and how one would tell the other, "you lost." While playing catch with the balloons, I wanted so badly to *'scream out loud, No—I Lost.'* I made decisions I can't take back and knowing I wouldn't be able to hear the sweet sounds of the three of them laughing and playing, made me want to cry and scream at the same time.

Tonight, I also listened to one of my good friends, Elizabeth, talk about all the mishaps in her life. She shared with me how her family members had a habit of disowning her because she joined the military, and how she'll miss a guy friend when it's time for her to leave for her tour overseas. While pouring out her heart, I found out that her coworkers also treat her indifferent because she's a little *different*.

I thought to bang my arm on the garage handle was bad, but sometimes, other people are going through worse things than you. She talked about just wanting to let out a loud scream.

I knew I had to find a way to reach her, saying, "You may not know this, but every time I talk to you, it's like therapy to me. Maybe you don't realize it, but you've helped me out a lot over the past six years."

She looked at me in awe and said, "For real?"

I said, "Of course you have." Then I told her that she's probably helped a lot of people over the course of years she's been here and didn't even realize it.

She replied, "You really think so." Then she smiled widely.

I knew right at that moment I had done what God sent me to do.

I realize I should stop screaming and start acting on things that mean the most—God, my family, my life. Everything else is not that significant, especially when I know without a doubt someone else is going through much worse.

I remember one night before going into work calling a friend of mine. I told him that I was trying to get in touch with his son via Facebook.

He asked me, "What message did you leave?"

I said, "Hello, my name is Donna Brown, and I need to speak with you about my son Stephen."

He said, "Ms. Brown. I am delighted to hear from you."

My friend laughed and said, "That was me."

Now I'm thrown because his son's face was on his Facebook page, but he was the one that responded. *Ooops!* Good thing I wasn't flirting or anything. Not that I would have been—being that I just left a relationship and wasn't trying to engage in another one that soon. However, after dating a guy four years my junior, I beg to differ. And I wasn't trying to raise him to be a man. Besides, the one who holds my heart makes everyone I've ever been involved with, stand back and take a second look at what a man is supposed to be.

There's only been one other man that made me stand up and say, "Now that's what you call a man, but he lives too far away to count."

Having a man that provides support, loves to engage in romance, and will take care of his family is vital to me. Those are a few aspects I look for in a man, and only a couple have come close.

If he can do any of these things, it's time to stop screaming out loud and grasp the moment for what it really is.

213

Chapter Thirty-Two

A Cry for Help

You watched them grow slowly inside the walls of your abdomen. Your body stretched in places you didn't know you had and yet, you delivered them into this world — pouring in sweat, screaming to the top of their lungs. Their bodies covered in so much goo and you think to yourself, now my life begins. You wake up in the middle of the night pulling out your breast or making them a bottle, changing their diapers, and if they are boys, we all know that if you don't remove the diaper carefully, you will on occasion get the yellow flow of urine straight in the face. You can't help but laugh because after all, you brought it on yourself. They didn't ask to be here, but you wanted to give your husband one of God's most precious creations—a child.

You comb their hair, clothed, feed, and cook for them until they can take care of themselves, and now your kids are at the age where no one or nobody can tell them what to do. They are smelling themselves and attracted to the opposite sex. They fall in love and you as a parent in their eyes don't know a thing about love because you're old and don't share the love they have.

Even if that were true, my love runs deep, and my passion for my children's happiness even deeper. I was proud when my oldest son Stephen received the National Merit Scholarship Award; ecstatic when he helped his school to win the national math competition in Toronto Canada by the National Society of Black Engineers. I was elated when he was accepted into Georgia Institue of Technology. I literally stayed in a marriage that practically ended in 2001 so my kid could finish high school with honors. Imagine my shock… when he told me, he would no longer need my assistance, or no longer plans to stay in contact with me because I tore the family apart.

When I decided to end my marriage in 2009, I sat with my family and told them how unhappy I was, and that I would be filing for a divorce. I wanted badly for someone to say something or try and stop me from hurting them. No one said anything. As time rolled along, I kept making them aware time was getting close, and if anyone had anything to say, to please let me know and we could talk about it. No one said a word. However, when the papers came in April 2010, I made everyone aware that the divorce was final.

I was devastated. I wanted them to fight for me…for our family, but they didn't. I decided to stay another six months until I could find a place for my youngest son and me to stay, and to help my ex with finances. But in the end, I was considered the one at fault.

Not that any of that matters at this point, but at the time, it did. Sometimes, we are taken for granted, and our spouses get set in their ways of doing things and forget about how we feel. Although we think it's okay to seek help from other family members, the best thing to do is seek help from professionals. If I could turn back the hands of time and think about the consequences my family faced with our divorce, I probably wouldn't. The simple fact is: I wasn't happy, and I wanted my freedom.

When people make promises to change the way they treat you, and things are still the same or worse, it's time to let go of the hurt and find peace within yourself. I did that and so happy God gave me the strength to do so.

My ex was a father to his children, but sometimes, the spouse needs a little bit of that love too. When you work all day, come home cook, clean, and help with the homework, you are exhausted. Sometimes, you just want to take a breather yourself. However, I wasn't that type of wife. I needed love from my husband, and he wasn't there to provide it for me. Whether it was a late night at work or travel for a month or so, when he came back, I needed him to be there for me.

I'm past that now because God gave me the ability to find myself and move on. That's what I plan on doing. I don't need a part-time husband; I need a man that will be there for me all times of the night, and when I'm at my lowest. Thank God for helping me find peace.

No matter what some women do, they tend to get a bad rap in life. We don't get the credit we deserve for helping our children, and sometimes spouses grow to become successful. Maybe that's why we cry for help when we've reached the end of our ropes.

Being told by your child that they'll never come back or don't care to see you again, is a slap in the face and it hurts. I don't recall raising any of my sons like that at all. I wholeheartedly believe working at night could have been part of the reason he felt like that. Having to stay with my ex-husband at night without me could have caused my oldest son to be angry. Or, maybe his father was bitter because we had built our family for over twenty years, and now it was gone. It still falls back to being loved, and if it's not there, then it's time to move on. I honestly believe if the following is not a part of my marriage, then I won't be:

- Romance – knowing how to embrace a woman without asking if it was okay.

- Helpful traits – Helping with the household chores and not laying around all day.

- Financial assistance – Being there for your wife when she'd stretched all her money and offering her a couple dollars on pay day.

- Support to his family – Understanding that he is married to you not his mother, brother, and sisters. Showing your wife and kids a little love instead of supporting his grown siblings.

- Trust – Learn how to trust and believe what your wife says is true, not other people.

All Grown Up

You raised them from a baby

And now they're all grown

You did your best for them

To provide them with a good home

You nurtured, fed, and bathe them

Putting them to sleep at night

But at times you often wonder

If all you've done made them turn out right

They're sassy, lazy, biggity, and hot around the collar

You often run around the house

Yelling, screaming trying not to holla

You make them clean their room

And beg them to take a shower

Seems like the more you do for them

You're pulling your hair out every hour

You can't help but love them

Cause they're a piece of your creation

If they don't stop being so stubborn and arrogant

They're going to ruin our entire nation

So you go to sleep at night

Hoping for a little rest

Then they come and lay beside you

Saying mom, I love you, you did your very best.

CHAPTER THIRTY-THREE

You Don't Have To Take It Anymore!

Many times in life we as women have to succumb to the ways of the world: rape, molestation, depression, adultery, you name it, we've been there. Then, we are told it's all in our minds—it's psychological, you brought it on yourself and so forth. But, why do we have to give in to the ways of the world? I'll tell you why. We as women but mostly African-American women are susceptible to pain. Our mothers, grandmothers, and aunts have gone through what we're going through and had to keep their mouths shut. You saw them bruised, beaten, and left for dead most of the times. They've been rejected, neglected, and subjected to hurt because their husbands or significant other chose another woman over them. They're left degraded and have to pick up the pieces.

But ladies, I'm here to tell you, there is a better way. Today you don't have to subject yourself to the pain, hurt, or the shame other family members endured. You are a much stronger woman. You have the power to stand tall and say, "I'm not going to take this anymore." You're bold, you're beautiful and self-reliant. You don't need a man to take care of you. You got your own money so be your best self. Stand up for what you want.

Ask yourself this, do you often find yourself alone wanting to be loved because your man is somewhere else? Have you as a woman changed your appearance to satisfy your man only to go unnoticed? Many times, women just like you and me live a life of loneliness, depression, and before you know it, some other man *mainly married ones*, comes around the corner of isolation and tells you all the things you want to hear. And before you know it, you're writing a book called, *Excuse Me Miss but I'm in Love with Your Husband*.

Now this is where it gets to be a little tricky. You found someone you just can't have. He's not yours. He doesn't belong to you. He belongs to another woman. Now, is it fair to interrupt someone else's marriage because yours is failing? No, it's not. Just because you're not happy doesn't mean you should make others feel the same.

You're not only living a "Secret Lie," but now you're engaged in a relationship with a married man, and you're under the impression he will leave his wife and kids for you.

CHAPTER THIRTY-FOUR

He's Not That Into You

(2010)

Ladies you have to remember that just because you want to be with a man, he may not want to be with you. You have to be ready for rejection. In saying this, how many times have you been so excited about seeing your man and he only wants to cuddle and watch TV? When was the last time he told you that he loved you and your heart skipped two beats? If this hasn't happened in the past week or so, face it, he's just not that into you.

Listen! Many women and on occasion some men go through the same thing. All I can say is *'been there, done that.'* Most alpha males, find it very hard to say the simple words that women love to hear. They say it doesn't mean anything. They're just words. Me personally, I need to be assured that I'm loved by the actual words being spoken to me.

So, that's exactly what I did. I used to tell this man how very much I loved him and waited forever for him to acknowledge that he loved me. Talking about needing a V-8 so badly, I ran to the kitchen and poured a tall glass of Hennessey…*kidding*! Then, went back to the room and started watching Soap Operas. That's how I felt about our relationship. It was just a Soap Opera going bad.

What's that all about anyway? I believe in my forty-three almost forty-four years of life, I have only had two men I could honestly say loved me. A few have tried, but only a couple could hold my interest. I mean (c'mon) let's be realistic! You don't want a man to sustain your time and then you find out he's only around to watch TV or take you to the movies. Then, when he finally finds interest in you, you're ready to move on with someone else.

So, let's take another trip together and see how you would handle this situation. You've been anxious about going over to his house. You and this guy have been seeing each other for over three years, but the problem is, he's married and has two small kids!

You send him a text, "Urgent, water running from my pipes, and I need you to come over and help me out."

He responds, "Can't help you! My wife is going through the same thing."

Now you're mad and frustrated. This man has promised you a lifetime of happiness, but he's still attached to his wife. The only thing you can think of is to go and take a cold shower and grab some chocolate ice cream. But it reminds you of all the times you've been with this guy, and you start to cry. Your ego is hurt, and your pride damaged. You just want to be left alone.

You suddenly get a buzz, and a knock comes to your door as you are sobbing like crazy. It's him. You scramble to wipe your tears away, but the hurt keeps coming. You let him in assuming he's there to apologize and make everything right again. He asks you to sit down. You know it can't be good.

He says, "My wife knows about you and wants to get rid of you. I called your name while we were…"

You stop him short of saying *'making love.'* Why is it they always have to share those types of things to mess up your day?

You reply with, "It doesn't matter anyway. I was about to let you know that I wasn't going to be with you anymore. I'm going to move on. Look for someone who really loves me. Besides, *I Can Do Bad All By Myself.*"

Now, his pride is hurt. He really wants to prove how much he really loves you, but you brush him off. "Why are you so upset? You knew I was married. You said you understood."

You smirk. "Yeah, I learned enough to know that I was a *fool* to keep letting you play with my mind. *I Love Me Better Than That*. I don't want or need a man that doesn't understand the true meaning of love."

Now, he is pleading for your forgiveness. "Augh, C'mon baby. Can I at least have a kiss goodbye?"

You cave and pretend to grab his face. "I said I don't want or need your type of love. Let me ask you one question. Have you ever loved me?" Shaking his head.

He just can't understand why you are so harsh. "I've always loved you. I just can't be with you all the time. If it were anyone else, I would leave them in a heartbeat. I just can't leave my wife and kids right now. Please understand. I'll make it up to you."

You politely move and tell him to get out of your house. You realize that he's not into you and never have been. He just wanted what he could get free of charge, no strings attached.

Now you've ticked him off, hurt his ego, and made him look like horse relish. He walks out the room slamming the door behind.

You laugh, and continue what you started earlier. But in all actuality, what did you expect, he's married, and you deserve better than that!

~

Ladies, can you honestly say you've been with a man that completely satisfied you first and himself second?

Okay, here's one more for you.

You go out on a date with this guy. You pick up the check. He's impressed. Sometimes, we have to initiate the first move before we get what we want. After several lunch and dinner dates, you're hoping for intimacy. When it finally happens, you are so relieved that you are calling him every single chance you get. Now, you're expecting that every time you get together whether it's his house or yours, you're gonna get the same reaction. Wrong.

You've been over his house three days and nights—spent the night over and he hasn't touched you. Now, you're saying, "What in the world is going on with this man?" You thought you were all that and dude just wants to give you a kiss. Nothing wrong with that, you think. Maybe he's trying to protect you and take it slow. You truly dig and appreciate his efforts. But you are also frustrated that he didn't even try. More than anything, you're determined to make this man notice you. You figure you would wear a cute black nightgown and see what happens. Absolutely nothing. He shook his head and said, "Baby, I have been working all day and to be frank, I have a massive headache."

Now you're embarrassed. You came to his house for what you thought would be a night cap and he has a headache.

Ladies, men do get them as often as we do. But the difference is most of the time we fake ours, so he will leave us alone.

As bad as you feel for him, you're thinking, *what the heck!* You're starting to second guess yourself wondering if it was something you said or if he doesn't like being with you. You're like a dog chasing his tail in his sleep. You try and forget that one and talk about it in a way you'd think he understands.

He grabs your hand and says, "I'll remember that next time we're together." Did I mention how frustrated that could make you?

Days even a week goes by, and you're tripping' again. He hasn't called or texted you. You're starting to feel like this man really isn't into you. Now you're mad. He tends to call when he wants to and come by whenever he's in the neighborhood. You thought you found Mr. Right but Mr. Wrong rather than Mr. Right is not into you at all. He wants you around for his convenience and not as a special friend. You send him a text and tell him that you'll see him in the next life.

Do you think men go through menopause too? I'd say so. They go through periods of 'it's just too overwhelming? Or? I've been with women my entire life. But they forget that when women are in their prime, they want and need to be loved. Sometimes we as women have to remind men that we need to be loved too.

Solution:

Sometimes waiting for the right man to come along can be a long process but in the end, when God is in the midst, He will show you the right man at the right time. Remember this: You don't have to settle for second best. God has your heart's desire waiting for you if you are patient enough to trust and believe it will happen. Marriages are sacred in God's eyes and it's not for us to tear them apart.

Listen: If a man is not into you, you would know. Look, there are so many wanton men waiting for the right woman to share their lives. If you do like I did, wait eight years or more for a man that wasn't into you, then you're crazier than I was. Life is too short to wait for what might be.

There may be several reasons a man might not be into you. A couple of them may include:

1. Narcolepsy.
2. He's gay.
3. He's on the down low.
4. He's married.

Whatever the problem may be, you have to accept it and move on with your life, knowing that your man will find you when you're ready to be a wife. Destiny is waiting for you.

CHAPTER THIRTY-FIVE

Men-O-Pause

(2011)

Ladies, let's face it. There's no getting around it, running away from it, or hiding from it. This thing, that will all of a sudden make you Snap, Crackle, and Pop—Pour into hot drenching sweats, and shaking like a frozen icicle is called *'Menopause.'*

One minute you're relaxing with some family and friends, the next minute you break out into tears. You feel the need to cuddle. You just don't understand. You've done nothing wrong, haven't offended anyone today or yelled at your kids. But suddenly, you feel the need to open up a can of *'whip your hinny'* on someone. That's *Menopause.*

Lately, I've been in tears not understanding why. I've been questioning my man about his love for me and finding a need to be held. I don't want to be alone not for one moment. Then it happened. While sitting at work on March 27, 2011, and suddenly, I'm coming out of my jacket. Everyone is cold but me. Usually, I'm freezing, but this night I'm sweltering. I want to take my clothes off and jump into a tub of cold water. Sweat is pouring down my legs and running down my back. Suddenly, I think, *'Oh my God! I'm forty-four years old. I must be going through Menopause.'*

But wait a minute! Shouldn't *Menopause* be a *'Pause from Men?'* What the heck is up with the sweat, tears, loneliness, and uncontrollable urge to mate like rabbits? As usual, *Menopause* is another word developed by men because he has no other word to use when his woman suddenly, snaps at him.

Merriam Webster's Dictionary says: *Menopause* is the natural cessation of menstruation occurrence usually between the ages of forty-five and fifty-five. Okay, hold up! *'The natural cessation of menstruation.'* What in the world is that? Really? C'mon! We all know that it's when the body decides to take a temporary or final pause from menstruation. Yeah, now it's time to get excited. No more pads, cramps, or bloating. Nor embarrassment from big bulky imprints in your pants.

But, if this is a relief, why all the hoopla? Though you may think it is over, some women forget all about protecting themselves. And then, mistake number seven is waving at you in your face saying, "Hey did you forget about me granny? Yep, you just got yourself a brand-new set of rules called, *'another baby.'* Just when you thought the coast was clear, Mother

Nature has sprung another surprise on you. So, while you are all excited about getting rid of your monthly, try containing those raging hormones as well.

Day two

I walked into work, and again I started pouring sweat. Now, I'm convinced that I'm *'Menopausing.'* But shouldn't I be taking a pause from men? Not in this lifetime! If I was the last woman on earth and no man was available, I would dig me one up from the grave and start from scratch.

When I attended, an event hosted by Danny Glover called, *Let Us Make Man*, I thought to myself, *"what's the purpose of making man if you can't have them when you want them?"* Some males want to direct your every move. But you should be the one taking control of your thoughts, mind, and body. After all, it's your body. It's up to you to tell it when, or when not, to take a pause.

Back in the day, a group called, *Klymaxx* sang a song called, *The Men All Paused* when they walked into the room. In this case, the men don't take breaks. They keep on coming.

Dramatization

You decide to tell your Husband that you are *men-o-pausing*, and you should take a break. He concedes hoping you would stay longer than you plan. You call your best girlfriend and ask if she would come along for the ride. You end up in Jamaica where the water is beautiful, the sun is beaming, the men are gorgeous, and yes, you are *men-o-pausing*…taking a break from the brothers, so you say.

'Yep, it's going to be a great week.' Two hours later, you are crying up a storm. Tears are streaming down your *face*…makeup that is. Your girlfriend hands you a tissue and asks, "Why the tears?"

You look at her with great intent and say, "I don't remember."

Now you're not only crying, but you can't remember why. You are *men-o-pausing* so badly that your memory is being lost.

She suggests you take a walk along the beach to jog your memory. Men appear from nowhere. Then you remember why you were crying. You are taking a pause from your man. Your hormones are raging, and you're hundreds of miles away from him. You see nice looking Jamaicans everywhere! That pause you were trying to take is no longer in effect. You want your man, and he's a few hundred miles away from your reach.

So, Sean Paul, a local resident walks over to you and says, "Now, what a beautiful woman like you doing all alone by yourself in Paradise?"

You scream on the inside. 'What is going on here? You can't touch only look. His tall, slender well-proportioned body is staring you in your face, and all you can say is, "I'm taking a pause from my husband."

He grimaces and looks around. "Augh, you're *men-o-pausing* as well. All the beautiful ladies come to see Sean Paul when they want a break from men—even their own husbands. Lemme give you a tour of my countryside. I can help you take your mind off your man. Come to my palace so I can rub your back and help you relax."

You start thinking, "Did he just say palace? Augh shucks! He's got money," You think, forgetting the fact that you're married and he's probably been with a whole slew of women.

Now you've gone from pausing to straight up greed. You think *Sean Paul* is going to pamper and treat you while you're in his beautiful country. But he has something else in mind. As you get ready to respond, your girlfriend grabs you by the hand and quickly pulls you back into reality.

"He just wants to take care of me," you try to explain.

"And all the other women *men-o-pausing* around here," she implies. "Look, girlfriend, we came here to take a break from men not to be picked up by the likes of Sean Paul."

Now you're fuming, frustrated, and confused. You want to flirt and wiggle every piece your Maker placed on your body.

"Can I just have fun this one time?" You ask.

Meanwhile, Sean Paul is smiling at you and waiting for you to say *'yes.'*

"No, not in your wildest dreams. Bring your hormone raging, hot steaming backside to your room."

You feel like your momma just scolded you and put you on restriction. You go back to your room, and your phone has been ringing off the hook. It's your husband, and he's been missing you as much as you've been missing him. He makes plans to meet you at your next port, but by the time his flight arrives, you've been sweating so hard he thinks you've been with another man. You try and explain that it's one of the backlashes of menopause and he laughs.

"You came here to get away from men, but you're surrounded by *fish* for the taking."

"I didn't order off the menu," you try to explain.

"So you're saying you're not here to have fun with other men?" Shaking his head like he knows better.

"Oooh no! I need a pause. I'm going through *men-o-pause.*"

"Sweetheart, Menopause is when your body goes through changes. You don't take a pause from your man. You're only taking a break from your body."

"Ohhhhh…" You sheepishly say dropping your head.

Since I have a concept of what menopause is, I wonder if some women experience it their entire life. I've watched the women I work with and see their bitterness, lack of confidence in themselves, harshness, and power they try to portray. If this is indeed menopause I am going through, it's my prayer not to turn out like some of my women associates.

CHAPTER THIRTY-SIX

Finding Donna Wright, Not Donna Brown

OCTOBER 23, 2010

On my journey *to* finding Donna Brown, I did not find her. Instead, I found Donna Wright, a happy but scared little girl needing to create other people to help ease her pain. The headaches suffered by Donna Brown are nothing compared to what Donna Wright had to endure.

Molestation, rape, loneliness, daily whippings'…you name it. Would I trade my childhood for the likes of the ones my children had—in a heartbeat? My boys have no idea what it feels like to get spanked with extension cords, switches, or race car tracks. They know what love feels like. I had no idea.

~

So, my husband and I are on the last leg of this incredible journey—bags packed with clothes to dine, at what I thought would be an elegant seafood restaurant. Ha! The joke was on us. We arrived at this seafood buffet at the Ocean Pacific Hotel in Tybee Beach only to find the price was $29 for Raw Oysters, dried out snow crab legs, steamed shrimp, fried hard clams, fish, and shrimp. The seafood salad looked like it had been sitting since earlier that morning.

No thanks! We decided to go downstairs to the sports bar, grab a menu, and watch some sports channels. The view from the window was marvelous. The Moon was full and glowing atop the rushing waves on the ocean front. I snapped a few pictures, then, ordered the seafood platter. Much better than my first choice—the so-called *buffet*. I ate fried oysters, fried shrimp, and a large piece of grouper fillet. Scrumptious was all I could say. Oh, how could I forget—the fried alligator tails! Oh my God! That was so good.

We sat in the curved window watching the rushing waves and tall sand dunes swaying across the white sand. The glow from the full Moon radiated through the tides as they started to settle around 7:00 p.m. The chill from the waterfront sent us back to our room to turn on the heater and watch TV. The evening was still young. I saw an article for the Diamond Casino in a magazine. My face lit up from the word *casino*. We jumped in the car and drove to the Diamond Casino that wasn't there. There were cars everywhere but no casino in sight. What the heck? Then it occurred to us that it was on a boat that set sailed at 7:00 p.m. It was now 8:37 p.m. and the ship had left the docks. *'Dang,'* I thought.

So there we were heading back, and it dawns on me we could play cards. We pulled into a Shell Gas Station, purchased a deck of cards, and a Sapphire and Gold Scratch-Off. We headed back to our room (1152) and begin playing Gin Rummy. For some reason or another, it reminded me of the days when my cousin Jennene used to kick our butts and leave us helpless.

We made a wager that if I won, he would have to give me a full body massage. Ummm, I just love his body massages. Anyway, I kicked his butt, and he rubbed my back, legs, thighs, toes, hands—you get the picture. I felt so loved. Afterward, we watched TV until the satellite kept going out. We decided to turn in and start the next day again. The strangest noise kept me up all night. What sounded like a motorboat proved to be a faulty air-conditioner unit. Man! He was knocked out, and I was tossing and turning all night. *"Bump the heat!"* I said and dashed towards the air-conditioner unit and shut it down. *Uhhhhh! Sweet relief!* Now, I can sleep.

Beep…beep…beep! "Augh, dang! It can't be the alarm," I murmured. I wanted to turn back over and sleep longer, but my dear husband had gotten up and sat on the side of the bed.

Then, I had a plan. It's only eight o'clock in the morning. "Would you like a back rub?" I asked trying to prolong the time.

"Well, I won't turn it down," he said smiling at me.

"Great," I replied putting baby oil on his back and listening to the Ahs and Ummms.

"I'm so exhausted," I proclaimed as I found myself lying backward on the white sheets with a dried blood stain. *Did I just say bloodstained?* Yep, I sure did, and it sure was. Not sure why I didn't have them change the sheets or give us another room. This room was the second one they had placed us in because the first one was cracked open, and the window latch was broken.

Nonetheless, I rested a few minutes. Then, we went to consume breakfast from the breakfast bar. Grits, eggs, and sausages. It was delicious along with the crescent rolls. We went back to our room, packed our stuff, and walked along the seashore.

That's when it all started. I wasn't finding Donna Brown or Portuguese, I found Donna Wright. As we walked along the side of the pier at Tybee Island, memories from my past flashed before me. Quietly, I could hear Otis Redding's *Sittin' on the Dock of the Bay,* and I smiled. Then told Terry what just gazed my mind.

'Hmmm,' he commented as we walked towards the pavilion for a breather.

After a good two minutes, I was ready to continue my journey. I said, "I'm going to walk up to the pier area. You can stay here if you're tired."

Immediately, he got up because he didn't want the guys to see me walking alone. It didn't matter, though. They still stared. I started back humming, "Sittin' on the Dock of the Bay watching the tides roll away. Ooh, sitting on the dock of the bay wasting time." I knew at that point Donna Brown or Portuguese was not who I was looking for, but Donna Wright.

Donna Brown was yet another person I created over nineteen years ago trying to find love. As I watched a fisherman and a woman cast their leads while participating in a fishing tournament, I wanted badly for it to be me. Then, I saw the most incredible thing—black dolphins.

"No way!" I proclaimed. I got so excited. I took pictures and made a video so my son would believe me.

When we reached the end of the pier, a gentleman was throwing back what I thought to be a *Stingray*. In reality, it was a *Skate*. Never heard of it. It reminded me of the time in life when I was roughly eight and a man I grew up with had caught a huge Stingray. After getting snatched around and popped, he let go of the fishing pole and let the Stingray go back out to sea. He was so mad. He lost his good fishing pole, and we cleared his path. 'Ever seen an enraged 'Big Bad Wolf lose his cool?' That was my pet name for a man that terrorized my family when I was little.

Minutes later, we walked back towards the pavilion, and there was yet another reminder of my childhood days—a fishing net. I smiled—then laughed out loud as I told my Terry about the time my stepfather, Mr. Potter was casting his net from the docks in Pensacola and threw himself into the water. It was a loud splash. Mama laughed so hard. Then, asked if he was okay. He chuckled as he made his way back to shore.

What great childhood memories! To be able to flash back to my childhood days were *priceless*. I wanted so desperately to find Donna Brown, but I apparently forgot that I didn't start out as Donna Brown but Donna Wright. There are so many memories I have tucked inside me, but as long as I'm able to remember the good ones, it's okay and a blessing.

Finally, I challenge each of you to look back into your life and find the memories and the determination you longed for. I guarantee, you will thank yourself for finding what you lost and what you have now found. Be blessed.

CHAPTER THIRTY-SEVEN

The Day My Life Stood Still

It was an ordinary day filled with excitement. Terry and me knew we had a long day's journey ahead of us, but I didn't care. We were heading to Maryland for the next four years getting away from the rhetoric of southern living and the cruelty of working at a place where the criticism comes from people who wears the same skin you wear. Terry tried his best to get us out of the move. He had no interest in going back to Maryland. But I persuaded him into going by telling him that God had something big for us there. He still wasn't convinced.

A brisk chill swept across the sky that Wednesday, the day of the move. The packers had left the previous day, and we decided to hang around, so that the carpet cleaners could clean the carpets for the new residents moving in.

After the carpets had been cleaned, we took another look around our large home and went to the garage where Terry's *Dark Knight* was parked. It was a name I gave his 2010 Black Camaro. How I loved that car! The neon lights facing the back wall beamed at me as I stared at him getting in it. I loved that car so much, but more importantly, I loved the man more than the car. As he sat on the plush leather seats, I shook my head wondering why he rarely drove that beautiful Dark Knight.

I headed to my silver *Mazda 6* parked on the streets, my bladder started to bother me. I had just left the bathroom, but I had to go *again*. I motioned to Terry as he began to back out of the garage and told him I had to go to the restroom. He shook his head and smiled.

"Okay baby," he said winking at me. "I'll be waiting for you right here." But he didn't stay in his car. He got out and started to do another sweep through the house. Everything seemed to be intact except for me whom he patiently waited for outside.

As I got ready to exit the bathroom, I heard a spiritual voice telling me, "Grab his hands and pray when you get outside!" I paused in my steps. The last time I had heard such a powerful voice like that was the night my mother and I were talking. The Holy Spirit spoke to me and told me to tell her that we needed to pray. I didn't question what I had heard, I told my mother we had to pray. It was the last time I spoke with my mom. She immediately suffered a stroke, aneurysm, and a heart attack after we got off the phone.

Five years prior, the Holy Spirit had spoken to me and told me to tell my mother, "If she didn't stop doing what she was doing (smoking), she wouldn't see her fiftieth birthday." She didn't listen to me and said that I must really hate her to say such words. I told her that one day she would find out just how much I really loved her. A month before her fiftieth birthday, she suffered a congestive heart failure.

I was terrified hearing that voice again. I didn't know what it meant or what it was insinuating. I really thought I was getting ready to lose a family member back home. I began walking towards the front door thinking to myself that I would pray in my car like I always do. But as soon as I reached the door to close it, the Holy Spirit was bold with me, *"Grab his hands and pray!"* I was scared to death panicking on the inside.

Terry looked at me and said, "Hope you can keep up!" Then turned to walk away but I grabbed his hand and said,

"Honey, we need to pray."

He looked at me with discernment. "Normally you pray when you get in your car."

"I know Honey, but we are going to be in separate vehicles, and this may sound strange, but I just heard a voice saying, "Grab his hands and pray!"

Terry looked at me strangely and said, "Okay."

So we stood right there in the middle of our yard, and I prayed like never before. I don't know what came over me, but I honestly believe the whole world could have heard me. It was loud, powerful, and very touching.

Terry gazed into my eyes and said, "Wow! I've never heard you pray like that before."

I said, "I've never heard me pray like that before." We never know why God have us do things, but it's not for us to understand. Just do it. I'm so glad I listened to God that day because I truly believe it changed the outcome of this whole story.

Once again, he said, "Hope you can keep up."

Our cars were packed to capacity with computers, monitors, clothes, valuables, and my well-loved Goldfish and Black Algae Fish swimming in their octagon tank. Our Rottweiler, Zeus had been given away three months prior because we had nowhere to keep him in Maryland. It really broke our hearts leaving him behind.

As we made our way to the next subdivision around from our house, water started to splatter, and I signaled for Terry to pull over. He got out of his car to assist me and stumbled dropping the light fixture and pump into the tank.

"Honey, are you okay?" I asked.

"Yeah, I just slipped and dropped the light. I'm fine." Terry told me.

"Well, don't kill the fish in the process," I jokingly replied.

We both smirked and drove off. As we approached the interstate, I felt the need to place a call to my Director, Donald Gray. I was in the process of producing another stage play in Augusta, Georgia, and he was helping direct it.

"Glad you finally got around to calling me back," he said. "Listen, we need to tighten up on a few things before the show.

Now…" he continued talking, but I had lost focus. Something wasn't right with Terry. He was driving very awkwardly.

"Wait!" I yelled seeing him swerve into the right lane, then suddenly back to the left almost hitting a red car. His car accelerated. I looked at my speedometer, and it read eighty-five. He was no longer driving seventy miles per hour. Terry had to be going over ninety, and I couldn't catch him. He was driving at that speed for approximately a quarter of a mile. I started screaming again.

"Donna, calm down," I heard Donald say but started screaming even louder.

"He's in the grass. Oh my God! Oh my God! He's gonna crash. He's going to hit that pole." I screamed loudly. The pole was one of those tall silver poles in the middle of the medium holding the green signs, letting you know what exit you are approaching.

"Nooooo," I screamed louder. "Terryyyyyyyy!" Then, he had crashed into that pole. It seemed like something out of a movie. People on both sides of the highway were in slow motion-sensing the impact of the accident.

Donald screamed for me to call 911 but I pulled into the grass and threw the phone on the seat. I could hear Donald still trying to call out to me. I don't remember parking the car. I didn't even turn the engine off or close the door. I just ran towards the car. Bystanders had beaten me to Terry. His car was demolished. He was crushed. I couldn't get to him fast enough. My heart was pounding, and I ran back to my car, turned it off, grabbed my phone, and closed the door. My knees caved on me. I couldn't make it to him.

Some men were standing at the car and yelled for me to stay back. "That's my husband," I yelled at them.

"You don't want to come over here," one of them said.

"Is he okay? I need to see him," I yelled. "We've called 911 already. Can we break the windows?" Another one asked. "Yes, please get my husband out of there," I told them.

Terry was trapped in his Camaro. The engine was sitting in his lap. His head was hanging down, and his eyes were closed. I really thought I had lost my husband that day. I knew God wouldn't bring us this far and let it all end like this. I just knew He wouldn't do that to us.

Emergency vehicles arrived within five minutes. People had already called before he crashed and the police, firemen, and ambulance from South Carolina were right there. We hadn't been gone more than fifteen minutes.

I took several pictures of the accident and immediately posted on Facebook. "This is my husband right now. Please pray for us."

I showed a picture of the car, the silver pole he had hit, and Terry in the car. Then, I called his daughter Stephanie crying trying to tell her what had happened.

She kept saying, "Donna, is my daddy dead?"

I replied to her, "I don't know. I don't think so."

She asked, "Where are you?"

I said, "Right before exit 5 on the South Carolina side of Augusta." Then I remembered that it was one exit before the exit I had placed in my latest book, *Loyal to Her Badge*, that was released in November 2015 on Amazon. The description of the accident in my book was almost identical to the one Terry had.

Terry held his head up after hearing me crying. He smiled, gave me a wink, and said, "I love you." Then he blew me a kiss.

I smiled, knowing that God had him at that point. It took the emergency crew over forty-five minutes to get him out of the car. His car was all over the place. The wheels were detached. The whole front end was smashed on the ground. He hit that pole so hard I just knew he was dead. I stood there shaking my head. I didn't understand. "Why Lord?" I asked. But then, I remembered what the Holy Spirit had told me to do.

"Grab his hands and pray!" Only God knew what was going to happen. I'm so glad that I was obedient. If I hadn't done what I was told to do, I wonder if the outcome would have been the same.

One of the officers was holding a rifle in his hands as I began talking to some of the guys who helped rescue my husband. "That's his paintball gun," I yelled at him.

The officer replied, "No ma'am. It's a rifle."

I was stunned. "My husband's a Police Officer. We were heading to Maryland for his job."

Then, they pulled out something that made me stop in my tracks. A bag filled with bullets and two cans of gasoline.

"Oh, my God!" That car was supposed to explode but God…my God said, "No. He's, my child."

As soon as I told them Terry was an officer of the law, everything changed. They worked feverishly taking good care of my husband. When they finally pulled him from that car, Terry yelled. The metal that sat on top of his left foot ripped his whole foot apart. Then Terry said nothing. He was in shock. They rushed him over to Georgia Regent University in Augusta where we had just left. He had a broken femur, and his foot was split wide open. But through it all, Terry survived. No one can tell me that God isn't good and He isn't merciful. I've been through a lot of deaths in my life but seeing my husband firsthand get into an accident, was the worst.

It's been six months and seven months since Terry's accident, and he's finally able to walk with his crutches. I don't know what I would have done if Terry lost his life, but I do know that with God, all things are possible!

That day, it all came to pass. I initially went on a journey over six years ago trying to find Donna Brown (my married name for nineteen years) but thought I had found Donna Wright (my birth name). God placed me in Terry's life so that we could find each other.

In essence, if I hadn't found Terry, I truly believe the outcome of his situation would have been devastating. I think God placed me in Terry's life to be his Angel just like He put Mrs. Clara Curry in my life when I was a little girl locked in that refrigerator.

I pray that we all can find our Angels, and in turn find ourselves for who God really wants us to be.

CHAPTER THIRTY-EIGHT

In Closing

The one thing I have discovered about myself during this process of finding me is that at the age of fifty, I still haven't fully reached adulthood. Take the time to find out who you are and what you want before you journey into another life that you might not be ready for. Find out who your friends are and aren't. The Bible teaches us not to put our trust in man but in the Son of God because man will most likely fail you. Watch what you say, who you say it to, and how you say it!

If you plan on telling someone your life story, prepare in advance for the world to intercept it. It won't be between you and the person you confided in anymore, but between you and the world.

Treat your friends how you want to be treated and leave an acquaintance as so. Never take personal life to work and work home. They don't mix.

If you're planning to leave your spouse, make sure you have grounds to do so before you decide, and for God's sake keep it to yourself. Telling the world doesn't make it any better.

Love with all your heart but don't lose your heart. Take nothing for granted when a vessel is broken, it can never be repaired by man. I realized that I am a broken vessel in need of the Potter to put me back together again.

So, a question I posed to myself, "Who are Donna and Portuguese and where can they be found?"

Chapter Thirty-Nine

Finally Found

Donna Wright

While trying to *Find Me*, I've come to realize that many obstacles have stood in the way of my dreams. I have allowed myself to believe that there is more to me than meets the eye.

I've created pseudonyms and nicknames for myself that would enable me to be other than the person I really am. I know deep down inside that I am a child of God and a very passionate, loving, kind-hearted person that have been rejected, torn, and taken advantage of throughout my life. But I don't dwell on it. I just deal with it.

If we allow ourselves to be partakers of the trials and tribulations we encounter, we would never be able to achieve our dreams, goals, or ambitions.

In writing this short story about my life and some fictional stories to stir your insides, I can honestly say that it has helped me gain self-control and power that I didn't think I had. It has been therapeutic as well as enlightening.

Honestly, I have to give credit to one of the ministers of my church. She encouraged me to seek out the person I was born to be. I never thought it would lead to this incredible healing tool. Thank you, Minister Ramona Adams of First Shiloh Baptist Church in Augusta, Georgia.

I told her that there are so many women that go around daily confused about who they are. It can be a dramatic experience, death, rape, incest, you name it.

For instance, the name Portuguese allows me to step outside Donna Hodges and be an entirely different person.

Portuguese (given at birth by my uncle David Wright) is a very friendly lady that loves to have fun.

Donna, on the other hand, is a passionate, loving, heavily into Christ kind-hearted person. Honestly, I don't think I have different personalities but the joy and excitement of playing the game of who you want to be that day, at that moment are priceless.

I have noticed one detail about me that was inadvertently left out. I am a loving, caring and self-giving person who loves to help those less fortunate and those that are weak and lonely. I may not have found out every facet of who Donna is, but I do know she is not a victim of circumstance, suffering from depression, or fearful of the Word of God.

I am the woman God created me to be your sister, a mother, and your friend.

God's Wrath

Obey my commandments is all that I ask
but yet, you tell a lie;
Make them a part of your daily task
or in your sins, you will surely die.

I will send storms a raging—
How the fierce lightning will strike;
Tumbling walls disengaging—
My roar you will not like.

I will make the calm sea rage—
Cause a cruise ship to sink;
Your sins must be disengaged
or I will come before you blink.

All the trees will disappear
like the echo lines of a clear blue sky;
My wrath will shake the ground that's near
before you can multiply.

Seek, and I will destroy
all that you hope to be;
the fires will burn the earth before
I will set you free.

Nation will rise against nation
The leaders they will fall;
Causing too much proclamation
trying to protect us all.

All I ask is that you abide
in my Word, so dear to Me;
My rage of thunder I will hide
if you fall on bended knee.

Donna "Portuguese" Hodges is an American author. She has been writing for over twenty years. Born and raised in Pensacola, FL, she grew up in the Pentecostal, Baptist, and AME churches. She graduated from Escambia High School in 1984 and joined the United States Navy as a Cryptologist. Though she wanted to excel as a Cryptologist, God had better plans for her life. Receiving Christ at the age of eight, she knew the Holy Spirit had been whispering in her ears and showing her things others will never see or could ever comprehend.

Though Donna has written other novels, she knew they were not appropriate in her life as a Christian. It was at that point that she realized God had given her a gift and she needed to do something with it. Immediately, God begin to use her to heal, pray, and minister to those around her.

In 2008, Donna wrote and produced her own stage plays, "I'm Sorry Momma," and "Steppin' Out." In 2013, she wrote and produced her most productive stage play, "Excused Me Miss but I'm in Love with Your Husband." which ran two separate times and was directed by Mr. Anthony Page (Augusta, GA) and Mr. Donald Gray (McDonough, GA). This stage play made its way to Pensacola, FL starring Mr. Gary Lil'G Jenkins (Silk) and Ms. Tamika Scott (Escape). Donna still couldn't find the growth she desired from God while working on things outside of her beliefs. It was during that time, the Holy Spirit whispered once again, "It's time."

She knew God was calling her for spiritual development and growth. While working on, "The Spirit that Dwells in Me," God instructed her to go into a field on the grounds of her church River of Life Worship Center on March 22, 2020. Being obedient and at the height of the pandemic, she obeyed and began looking into the sky. Knowing others would not believe what she saw that day, God placed witnesses to account for her testimony in church. They were amazed by what she spoke while standing in the pulpit one Sunday. Now imagine God allowing Donna to see straight into the Sun with her naked eyes and showing her a crystalized sword that turned into a cross, two darkened figures on the right side of the Sun, and a brass altar with three poles on the left! Almost sounds too good to be true right? Well, it happened to her, and it changed her life forever.

One of the most rewarding experiences in her life was working on, 'The Spirit that Dwells in Me." She believes that it has taught her that the true gifts of the Holy Spirit are trusting and believing God can and will do the imaginable. When Donna asked God, "Why me?" His response to her was, "Why not you?" And that has made all the difference in her life. Through dreams and prophecies, God has opened her heart and is expanding her gifts for the world to see. Donna has never taken for granted what God have blessed her with. Neither does she boast about the things that come easy for her. She continues to praise and worship God through song, giving, and being a witness for Him.

To be the first to know about Donna's new books & movies, visit her website at, **http://donnahodgesauthor.com.**

Thank You for Your Purchase.

If you enjoyed this book, please post a review on the platform where you purchased this book or scan the QR Code to post a review on Amazon. Thank you.